Finding Destiny

Serena K. Wallace

NEW LIGHT
PUBLISHING COMPANY

This is a work of fiction. Names, characters, places, and incidents either are the product of the author's imagination or are used fictitiously, and any resemblence to actual persons living or dead, business establishments, events, or locales is entirely coincidental.

FINDING DESTINY

A NEW LIGHT BOOK published by arrangement with the author

PRINTING HISTORY
NEW LIGHT EDITION / JANUARY 2006

For information address:
New Light Publishing Company
P.O. Box 2331
Edmond, OK 73083-2331

ISBN: 0-9777120-0-1
LCCN: 200692019

PRINTED IN THE UNITED STATES OF AMERICA

Finding Destiny is dedicated to those who know they are not perfect, but try anyway. Nothing is too great for God's forgiveness.

Acknowledgements

First, I want to thank my husband Lonzo, whose love and unyielding support gave me the courage to write and publish this book. You are my best friend, and I love you with all of my heart and soul. To my mom, Kathleen Custis, I thank you for telling me that I was special until I believed it. I am who I am because of you. To my daddy, Charlie Custis, I love you, and I live to make you proud of me. I hope I've done a good job so far.

I want to send love to my brother, Brian, and give thanks to my wonderful friends and family who read my book and gave great feedback. Thanks for your prayers and encouragement.

But most importantly, I thank God for His son Jesus, without whom I would not be.

Finding Destiny

The Promise

God must be so disappointed in me. Those were the first words that crept into my guilt-stricken mind as Damian placed a kiss on my cheek and rolled his moist, naked body off of mine. He shifted onto his side and leaned on his elbow, resting his head in the palm of his hand.

"Are you all right?" he asked, as he reached for my face and gently caressed it with his fingertips. I turned my face toward him and forced a peaceful smile.

"Yeah. I'm okay," I answered, almost at a whisper. I wasn't okay, though. From the depths of my 20-year-old soul, I wasn't okay.

"I didn't hurt you, did I?" His question exuded concern.

I sent him another fake smile to ease his worry and murmured, "I'm fine."

Damian pulled me closer to him and I buried my face into his chiseled chest, still sticky with sweat.

"I love you, Destiny. You know that, right?"

"I know. I love you, too."

Even as I said the words, I began to drown in the reality that I had just given this man everything I had - my heart, my trust...now, my body - my body that had never been given to another man - the body I had planned to save for the one I married. I tried my hardest to curb this sudden surge of vulnerability, wrapping my arms around Damian as tightly as I could, holding on for dear life. I needed him now. He was a part of me. But something inside just didn't feel right.

"What's the matter, Baby?" he asked, as tears leaked from my eyes onto his bare skin. Damian's hand gently stroked away a tear from my cheek and forced me to look at him.

"I don't know," I sniffed. "I guess I'm just happy being here with you."

A blind man could see through my lie. But Damian just hugged me close to him again and pressed his round lips into kisses all over my face.

"You know I want to marry you someday, right?" he asked, between kisses. "When I finish law school, we'll get married, buy a house, have kids…the whole nine," he added, with an air of optimism. "You're the only woman I want."

I smiled and reciprocated his affection as if his words were exactly what I wanted and needed to hear. Before long, Damian's kisses became more and more passionate and ignited the feelings that led us to bed in the first place. As we made love again, I strained to push them away - the words in my head that kept haunting and taunting me. "You broke your promise. This is not your husband."

CHAPTER 1

Modern-Day Supremes

My mother said she named me Destiny because God had extraordinary plans for my life. She always told me I was special, but I never knew why I would be any more special than anyone else. Somewhere along my young journey, though, I actually began to believe her.

I thought about how much I looked like my mother as I stood in front of my bathroom mirror, plucking my eyebrows and examining the imperfections of my toffee brown skin. Even with all my flaws, I was proud of the young woman staring back at me in the mirror. She had come a long way from her days as a bony little girl with big teeth, who was too shy to look people in the eye. Now, that bony little girl was all grown up.

I had spent the last four years balancing classes, term papers and exams with healthy doses of parties, road trips and hanging out with friends. By the grace of God, those four years culminated into graduation and a bachelor's degree in journalism from the University of North Carolina. My parents and older sister drove down from Virginia to celebrate with me and beam smiles of pride as I ran across the football field with the other thousands of graduates. Now, the dust from the pomp and circumstance of graduation had settled, and I was alone in my humble apartment getting ready for one last night out in my college town.

My hair: fresh from the salon. My perfume: intoxicating. My dress: sexy, but classy with the perfect shoes to match. When my reflection met my approval, I gave myself a sassy wink before heading back to the bedroom to hunt for my tiny black clutch purse. In the middle of my search, the phone rang and I answered, "Hey, Girl," without even looking at the caller I.D. I knew it was either Vanessa or Janel.

"Hey, D.," said Vanessa. "Listen, I need to borrow your brown-strappy sandals. The ones I wore last time, remember?"

I rolled my eyes sarcastically.

"Nessa, please tell me you're not wearing that same outfit again. You need to give it a rest."

"Whatever, Girl," she said. "Don't hate me because I'm beautiful. Besides, it's the best thing I've got going in my closet."

"Wear what you want," I said laughing. "I just need you two heifers to be ready when I get there. If we're late, you're paying my way in."

I discovered my clutch and began filling it with the contents of my everyday purse as Vanessa continued.

"We'll be ready, Girl. Just bring the shoes!"

"Okay! I'm leaving now so be ready."

I hung up the phone and grabbed Vanessa's requests out of my closet. I took them to the kitchen and found a plastic bag in the pantry to put them in. With the bag, my keys and purse in hand, I left my apartment, locking the door behind me.

It was a beautiful early summer evening, and a warm breeze kissed my face as I walked to my car. I felt good. It was as if this night marked the end of one chapter of my life and the beginning of another. I hopped in my Altima, cranked it up and turned up the volume on the radio a few decibels louder than necessary. I sang and danced in my seat while I drove up the highway to Vanessa and Janel's apartment complex. After a quick ten-minute drive, I pulled up to my friends' building and approached the door where more loud music thumped through their stereo. I pounded hard on the door and a few seconds later, Vanessa opened it wearing nothing but a black bra and a towel wrapped around her tiny, muscle-bound waist.

"Hey, Girl!" shouted Vanessa over the music as she popped and swung her hips to the beat. "This is my song!"

"How about you save those moves for later on tonight," I ordered playfully, as I entered the apartment and handed her the shoes in the bag. "I knew you two wouldn't be..."

I glanced over at Vanessa, and before I could finish my sentence, I broke out laughing at her homemade dance routine - a rendition that would give any BET video girl a run for her money. She was so crazy!

Vanessa, born and raised in North Carolina, was my first glimmer of southern hospitality when I first moved from Richmond, Virginia to the Tar Heel State. I met her during freshman orientation when she offered to help me and my sister lug suitcases and boxes into my college dorm room. The first things I noticed about Vanessa were the deep dimples tucked in her chocolate brown cheeks that accentuated her bright white smile. She stood five feet tall with an athletic build, and she wore a short, stylish haircut that she could never maintain without the assistance of a hairdresser.

Vanessa was a sociology major who graduated with a 3.8 GPA and had a job lined up with a non-profit organization called Sisters on the Rise. She loved working with young girls in the community, and her goal was to get as many young, black girls into college as possible. It was actually pretty funny to see Vanessa so serious about her work because most of the time she was silly and fun-loving.

"We're gonna paaaarty! We're done with cooollege!" Vanessa whooped in a singsong melody, almost dancing out of her towel.

Unavoidably taken in by Vanessa's excitement, I indulged my own craziness and danced along with her. We both slid into a series of old-school dances, from the Kid-N-Play to the Running Man, laughing the whole time. I decided I'd better stop before I sweated out my hair and made my feet hurt prematurely.

"I'm gonna see how Big Butt is coming along," I said, referring to Janel. "You need to hurry and get dressed so we can go!"

Vanessa turned the music down a notch and went back to her

bathroom to finish getting ready. Meanwhile, I took my good mood and dance moves down the hallway to Janel's bedroom, where I found Janel in shorts and a t-shirt, sifting through clothes in her closet.

"I should've known *you* wouldn't be dressed," I smirked, standing in the doorway, hand on hip. "I'll tell you like I told Vanessa. If we don't get there in time, you're paying my way in."

She ignored my comment and made a wicked face.

"Don't *you* look cute tonight?" Janel sneered. I spun around like a model.

"Yes. I do."

"Not as cute as *I'm* gonna look in about five minutes." Janel whipped around and continued rummaging through her closet. "I just need to find something to wear. My butt is spreading and I can't fit anything in this stupid closet," Janel said in disgust.

Whatever she put on, I knew she would look fabulous in it. Janel was one of those dangerously attractive women that other women loved to hate. She had the skin color of warm butterscotch, doe-like brown eyes, long relaxed hair, full lips – and let me not forget to mention her voluptuous chest and a behind that could make a blind man see. I wouldn't call myself an envious person, but if I was, Janel would be number one on my hit list.

Most people, girls and guys alike, were intimidated by Janel's good looks, so it was difficult for her to make friends. One day during freshmen year, Vanessa and I were hanging out in the dorm lounge when Janel decided to approach us. She asked if we'd like to ride to the mall with her, and since she was one of the few freshmen girls who had a car on campus, we jumped at the chance to get away for awhile. Soon, Vanessa and I learned that Janel was really sweet and funny beneath her tough exterior and we grew to love her.

Janel was in a five-year nursing program, which meant she had one year left to finish before she graduated. Needless to say, the evening was not as significant for her as it was for me and Vanessa. Yet, Janel never passed up an opportunity to go out.

"Well, this will have to do for tonight," I said, noticing a simple red dress lying across the bed. I handed it to Janel. She held it up, and visions of how gorgeous she would look in it danced in her eyes.

"This might actually work," she said amazed. "Yeah! I'm gettin' me some tonight!" she exclaimed, while she bopped her shapely figure around the room.

It was after 11 p.m. when Vanessa and Janel were finally ready to leave. We drove together to this semi-upscale nightclub in Janel's brand new black Expedition. The SUV was a guilt gift from her father, who had come in and out of Janel's life like a cold ever since her parents divorced almost ten years ago. As long as Janel's dad showed up with a gift, he easily won her forgiveness for his absence.

Our parking space seemed like it was miles away from the front door of the club, but we strutted up to the entrance looking like the modern-day Supremes. Our fitted dresses, glossy lips, high-heels and swinging hips made a few heads turn as we merged into the long line of club-goers. The three of us joked and laughed as we waited in line, eyeing all the women who were trying way too hard to be sexy and rolling our eyes at the men showing off their rimmed-up cars, blasting music as they drove through the parking lot.

The place was packed. The D.J. was playing the latest Rap and R&B chart-toppers, which meant the dance floor was packed, too. Not long after we all eased our way through the crowd and took up any bit of space we could find to dance, some alcohol-breathed ape invited himself to press his pelvis up against my behind. I politely made some space between us, but allowed him to dance with me, even though I despise the smell of alcohol breath. I waved my hands over my head, twisted my hips and lost myself in the music. I might as well have been dancing in that room by myself.

After about three songs, I motioned to Vanessa and Janel that I was heading to the ladies' room. Vanessa joined me so she could ditch the bugaboo she was dancing with.

"Baby, you lookin' good. Can I talk to you for a minute?" said some random guy standing by the wall. I ignored him and grabbed Vanessa's arm, rushing her into the bathroom.

"It's like a freakin' meat-market in here," I said, as I grabbed a paper towel to pat the sweat from my face.

Vanessa laughed at my comment as she positioned herself in front of a mirror beside me. We fluffed our hair and reapplied our lipstick as loud bursts of music flew in behind each lady who entered restroom – one of which was an acquaintance of ours from college named Carmen. We used to live on the same floor in the dorms during freshman year.

Carmen outfitted her five-foot-nine-inch frame with high heels, blue jeans and a halter top that left nothing much for the imagination. She flashed a winning smile and flipped her long braids over her shoulder as she sashayed into the room.

"Heeeeey!!!" We all shouted once we recognized each other. The three of us exchanged hugs.

"I am loving your outfit," Carmen said to Vanessa, as they released their hug.

"Thanks, Girl!" Vanessa exclaimed.

She shot me a look that said, "See, it doesn't matter how many times I wear the same outfit if it looks good on me."

I just shook my head, and Vanessa danced off into one of the stalls to use the toilet.

"So, Destiny, what are your plans now that you've graduated?" Carmen asked me.

"I'll be working as a photographer for the *Baltimore Sun*."

"Go, Girl. I hear that the Maryland, D.C. area has lots of fine men with good jobs!"

"We'll see!" I said, laughing. "What are your plans?"

"Girl, I got accepted into Carolina's law program."

"Good for you!" I said, genuinely excited for her.

"Hey, is Damian still in law school? Maybe he can give me some advice on how to survive the next four years," Carmen joked. But just hearing his name deflated my good mood.

"Yeah, he's still in for now," I said, despondently.

"Maybe I'll ask him about it. He's here with you, right? I think I saw him by the bar."

"You saw Damian here?" I asked, stunned but trying not to show it.

"Yeah. You two are still together, right?" Carmen asked optimistically.

"No, not anymore."

Just then Vanessa stepped out of the bathroom stall.

"Don't you dare get all dry on me, Destiny," she said, stepping to the sink to wash her hands. "We're going to have a good time whether he's here or not."

"Oh, I'm so sorry!" Carmen gasped, obviously regretting that she had brought up Damian's name. "I didn't know you two weren't together anymore."

"No, it's okay. I'm cool with it," I lied.

"Don't even worry about him, Girl," she said, trying to recover. "You're gonna have plenty of men to choose from up in Baltimore, Baby!"

I laughed with Carmen on the outside, but my insides were twisting as I thought of Damian in the other room.

Vanessa and I made our grand entrance back into the club and the music helped me regain my composure. I eyeballed the dance floor for a cutie to help me keep my mind off Damian. But wouldn't you know it? Who did I see rocking back and forth with some yakky-weaved girl? Yep. Damian.

As we weaved through the mass of sweaty bodies in motion, I tried to avoid looking around too much for fear of running into him. But our eyes met inevitably. I looked away quickly and followed Vanessa to the other side of the dance floor where we slipped into a comfortable dance and tried to ignore cat calls from men standing on the wall.

"You all right, Girl?" Vanessa asked in my ear so I could hear. "I see you looking for Damian."

"No, I'm not looking for him," I lied shyly. "And quit saying his name."

"Well, he's looking for you. I think he's trying to come over here."

A queasy feeling erupted in my stomach. Why did this man make me so sick? If I was honest with myself, I would have admitted that I wanted Damian to come over. He was like a drug that made me feel so good, but let me down so hard.

Vanessa and I continued dancing, although any minute I was expecting to feel Damian's arms wrap around my waist. But he didn't come. In fact, I didn't even see him on the dance floor anymore.

Instead, I found Janel who hadn't stopped shaking her tail on the dance floor since we arrived. She sauntered over to me and Vanessa who had found new dance partners.

"Hey, Ladies!" yelled Janel, as she bumped her hip against mine while holding a drink in her hand. "The men in here tonight are weak!" She took a sip of whatever it was she was drinking.

I was suddenly caught off guard by the very thing I was expecting just a few moments earlier - Damian's hands on my waist. I turned around abruptly ready to smack whatever loser thought he had free reign to touch me.

"Relax, Baby. It's me," Damian said, with a glistening smile. He hugged me up in his arms and our sweaty faces touched. His shirt was damp from perspiration, but he still smelled good. And I was glad he didn't have alcohol breath.

"Ladies, I need to borrow her for a little while," he said to Janel and Vanessa, who looked ready to maul Damian as soon as I gave the nod.

"I'll be back in a minute, okay?" I said. I tried to sound as if it would be all right, but I wasn't sure it would be.

I held on to Damian's waist and buried my face in his back as he plowed a tunnel through the hot mob to an empty space on the dance floor.

"You're the finest thing in here, you know that?" he said in my ear as we danced.

I ignored him and tried to pull off my sexy/classy dance.

"So," Damian continued. "How have you been? It's been a long time since we've talked."

"I'm good," I answered in a carefree tone.

"So, what's up? What are you gonna do now that you're a college graduate?"

"I'm the newest photographer for the *Baltimore Sun*," I said with pride.

"Baltimore? Baltimore, Maryland?"

"Yes, Baltimore, Maryland! Do you know of any other Baltimore?"

"I just thought you were trying to stay here," he said. "Didn't you have that internship last summer with the newspaper in Raleigh?"

"Yeah. It helped me build my portfolio and land my position at the *Sun*. My sister just moved up there, and I'll be staying with her."

"Baltimore," he repeated in astonishment. "I can't believe you're trying to leave me, Woman."

"Whatever, Damian. What about you? How's law school coming?"

"It could be worse. I don't know if I'm feelin' law school anymore, but we'll see how it goes."

"Yeah."

"Baltimore, huh? Are you sure you want to move way up there? I'm gonna miss you."

The truth was that I was going to miss him, too. But I wouldn't dare say it.

Damian and I danced through one more song without conversation then I told him I was going to meet back up with the girls. The longer I stayed with him, the sadder I became. So, I pecked him on the cheek before I walked away, not giving him a chance to protest my leaving. I glanced back to see him standing there, watching me. Then I noticed three vultures on the sidelines that had been waiting to back their butts onto him all night. *You can have him*, I thought to myself.

When I finally caught up with Vanessa, I discovered that the modern-day Supremes were minus one. Janel had found the lucky man for the evening and followed him back to his place, leaving us without a way home. I knew we shouldn't have let her drive. She had a bad habit of doing that. Luckily, we ran into Carmen and some of her friends in the parking lot and caught a ride home with them.

Serena K. Wallace

CHAPTER 2

Through this Song and Dance

Despite the less-than-perfect ending to my last night out with the girls, I woke up the next morning on cloud nine. My first thoughts were that my college career was over, and in a few days I would be leaving my very familiar surroundings and heading off to find my destiny – whatever it may be.

With a slight bounce in my step, I headed to the kitchen and whipped up two eggs, two pieces of bacon and a slice of toast. I enjoyed a leisurely breakfast while watching my favorite show, the Golden Girls. Although I had seen the episode 80 million times, I watched as though it was the first, and I still managed to laugh out loud during all the funny parts.

After rinsing my dishes and brushing my teeth, I began my day's goal of packing my belongings for the big move. I worked until about three o'clock before I decided to check on Vanessa and Janel.

"Hey, Girl," Vanessa said, answering the phone.

"Hey. Did Janel make it home okay?"

"Yeah. But I'm not speaking to that selfish cow for a week," Vanessa snapped. "You packing?"

"Yeah."

"Need some help?"

"No, I think I got it. What are you up to?"

"I'm about to go see Rodney. I don't want to be here when Janel decides to come out of her room because I might slap her." Vanessa was serious, but I laughed. "I'm not kidding, D.," she said. "She loses her mind when she gets around men and I hate her when she gets like that. How could she leave her friends at a club with no way to get home? She's pulled too many stunts like that and I'm tired of fooling with her."

"You know how she is, Vanessa. She's grown and she's gonna do what she wants to do."

"Her ways are gonna catch up to her one day. You watch and see," Vanessa said, sounding like somebody's grandmother.

"I know. I'll talk to her. I may stop by tonight after I pack a few more things."

"Well, I probably won't be here. I'm about to leave now," Vanessa said.

"Okay. I'll talk to you later."

"Bye, Girl."

"Bye."

Janel, Janel, Janel. That girl was something else. I don't know how she picked up this habit of using men to escape whatever problem she had. If she was broke, she'd smile in the direction of a man with money. If she was feeling hot and bothered, she would smile in the direction of a man with money and hope he was good in bed. I just prayed that her sexual escapades didn't end up costing her more than she was willing to pay.

I'd decided to check on Janel later that night, but the better part of my Saturday was spent listening to music while neatly arranging all my books, knick-knacks, dishes and clothes into boxes I had rallied up from the grocery store. I had just finished boxing a set of dishes when I heard the faint ringing of the phone under the sounds of my music. I skipped into the living room to turn down the volume on the stereo, and then darted back to the kitchen to answer the phone.

"Hello?"

"Hey, Baby," crooned the deep voice on the other end.

"Hey." I sounded mildly surprised as my insides turned into a mess. The voice on the other end of the phone was none other than Damian.

"What's up?"

"Nothing really," he answered. "I just wanted to see how you're doing."

"I'm fine."

"I know. That was pretty cold leaving me on the dance floor by myself last night."

"I'm sure you weren't lonely for too long."

"I'm not worried about anybody but you, Baby."

"I seriously doubt that."

"I want to see you before you leave," he said, changing the subject. "Can I stop by sometime?"

"Um. I don't know." I tried desperately to think of any believable excuse for not meeting him. "I'm supposed to meet up with some friends tonight." I bit my bottom lip and prayed he wouldn't press the issue.

"All right," he said. "I'll give you a call tomorrow, then. I really want to see you."

"Uh huh. I'll talk to you later."

"Love you, Baby."

"Bye, Damian."

Anyway, I thought to myself as I hung up the phone. I made myself snap out my daze and tried to regain the sense of euphoria I had before Damian's call. It didn't work.

The clock read 6:35 p.m. when my packing was interrupted by the sound of hunger rumbling in my stomach. I hadn't eaten since breakfast, so I decided to run to Subway or Wendy's for dinner before I stopped by Vanessa and Janel's place. I slicked my hair back into a low ponytail and changed into a pair of jean shorts, a light blue shirt and a pair of over-priced flip-flops. Then I quickly brushed my teeth and grabbed my purse off the coffee table.

I was fumbling around in my purse for my car keys when I heard a knock on the door. I went to it and peeked out of the peephole, but someone's finger was covering it up. I had a feeling it was Damian standing on the other side.

My heart sank. I lost every ounce of cool in my body and my legs got weak. Before I opened the door, I smoothed my hair and moistened my lips. And there he stood, looking sexier than ever. Why did he look so much better now that he wasn't mine anymore?

"Hey," he said. "I'm sorry I didn't call before I came. I was hoping to catch you before you went out with your girls."

I couldn't help but watch his round lips when he talked. Oh, how I missed those lips.

"Are you about to leave now?" he asked.

"No, come on in. I'm not meeting my friends for a little while."

I widened the door and let Damian come inside, feeling a zap of electricity as he brushed by me. We both took a seat on my couch and awkwardly waited for the other to say something.

"I'm sorry to drop in on you like this. I just wanted to check you out one more time before you left," Damian said, as he rested his elbows on his knees and clasped his hands together.

"It's fine. Really. You just caught me in the middle of packing, so excuse the mess."

"Your place is always clean, Girl," he said, with a cattish grin.

I returned the smile half-heartedly.

After an uncomfortable moment of silence amplified by Damian's penetrating stare, he finally said, "I'm gonna miss you, Baby. I know things didn't work out so well between us, but maybe I can visit you and we can hang out sometime. I don't know what I'll do if I can't see your pretty face."

I didn't know what to say. I hoped he didn't want me to say I would miss him, too – even though I would. I was actually looking forward to moving on with my life without him, but a small part of me still wanted things to work out between us.

"Come here," he said, holding out his hand.

I sighed, quivering just at the thought of his touch. I reached out my hand to take his, knowing how good it would feel to hold him, and how much it would hurt when he left.

We had been through this song and dance many times before and always ended up at the same place. But something inside me wanted to go there one more time. I let him take my hand and draw me to him as we both stood to our feet. Damian gently pulled me close to him, and I rested my head on his chest, breathing deeply and wrapping my arms around his slim frame. The smell of his cologne took me back to the first time we met and how happy I had been with him.

My mind drifted back to when I first met Damian. It seemed like just yesterday when I was a bright-eyed, wonder-filled college freshman who admired him from afar. He was the fast-running track star whose good looks earned him a steady flow of fans and female attention. I was the shy, aspiring photographer who caught his eye while taking pictures during one of his track meets. Fast-forward six months later, and we were inseparable. That is, until I was faced with a dilemma.

On one hand, I could either honor my promise to myself and to God that I would save my virginity for my husband, or indulge every fiber of my being that wanted to make love to Damian, who I really thought would be my husband one day. I chose the latter. Little did I know that that fateful moment would mark the end of our fairytale courtship and the beginning of a never-ending emotional rollercoaster ride.

"I hate you," I said softly as I enjoyed the sensation of Damian's fingertips caressing the skin on the small of my back.

"No you don't," he whispered. "You don't hate me."

Damian leaned toward me and gave me a series of deep, delicious kisses that tasted like sweet pieces of candy. I almost lost my breath. I felt so comfortable with his touch and the familiar jolts of excitement that charged throughout my whole body when he kissed me. But even as I let him run his hands over my hips and thighs, I knew in the back of my mind that he had to leave.

"What are we doing?" I said breathlessly, as he kissed my ear and down my neck. I gently tried to push him away.

"Anything you want, Baby."

He draped me with more kisses.

"Wait. Wait a minute," I said, slowly moving myself away from him.

"What's wrong?"

"I can't keep doing this with you," I said sadly. "I can't keep letting you come in and out of my life. This just isn't working for me anymore."

Damian frowned and stood there with his hands in the pockets of his loose jeans. He lifted his hand to his mouth and smoothed his perfectly groomed goatee before speaking again.

"I don't know what you want from me," he said, sounding defeated. "I'm just trying to be with you and here you go again, making this relationship difficult. Why does everything have to be so serious with you all the time?"

"Damian, we've been doing this for too long, and I'm just tired of fighting to make this relationship work when we're clearly not on the same page."

"How long are you going to keep playing this game with me?"

"Game? What are you talking about?"

"You know what I'm talking about," he said, slightly frustrated. "First you say you're ready to take our relationship to the next level. And now that we did, you want to wait until we're married before we make love again. It's like you're dangling sex in front of me so I'll marry you, and I'm not ready for that right now."

"You're ready to sleep with me but you're not ready to marry me, right?" I asked accusingly.

"See, there you go again; dangling sex in front of me!"

"I'm not dangling anything in front of you! I told you why I wanted us to wait and you said you understood."

"What difference does it make now? You know I love you. What else do you want?"

"I want us to be right! I want our marriage to be blessed! I know we're not perfect, but we at least have to try, Damian. Now, I'm willing to accept that you're not ready for marriage, so why can't you accept that I'm not ready to continue a sexual relationship with you until we're married?"

"This isn't even about us 'being right.' It's about you controlling me like you try to control everything else in your life. Well, I'm sorry that I'm not working on your timetable."

"I can't even believe you would say that to me!" I snapped. "You think I'm using the Bible to manipulate you into marriage! You have no idea how hard this whole thing has been for me. You don't know me at all. How could you say that?"

"Look, I'm sorry," he said, in an effort to deflate the intensity of our conversation. "I know this spiritual thing is important to you, but..."

"You said it was important to you, too! So why are you acting like I'm trying to be holier than thou?"

"I just think God knows I love you and I want to be with you more than anything. I really do want to marry you, Baby. Just not right now."

"This is not a game to me. I shouldn't have to choose between you and what's best for my spirit. I'm so tired of wasting my tears on you."

"Waste? Is that what you think I am after all we've been through? That's what you think of our relationship?"

"That's not..."

"Look, Destiny," Damian interrupted. He stepped toward me and clasped my hands with his. "You know I care about you, all right. I love you to death. But I can't promise you a big house and picket fences right now. There are some things I have to do for myself before I get married."

"I didn't ask you for a house or fences! I didn't ask you for anything!" I yanked away from his gentle grip as a hot rush of anger came over me. "Why did you even come here?" I asked, steaming. "We haven't been together for six months and now that I'm leaving, you have the nerve to show up here and stir up drama?"

"Maybe I shouldn't have come here," he said coldly as he got up and walked toward the door.

"Maybe you're right!"

Damian stopped just short of the door.

"I don't understand you," he said, with his hand resting on the door knob. "Tell me what you want. What do you want me to do? I don't want to leave here like this."

"I don't know. I think I just need to be alone. I need you to leave me alone for awhile because...I just. I'm just tired of going back and forth. It's draining me," I said, tears welling up in my eyes.

"Don't cry, Baby. I'm sorry."

Damian inched toward me, but I raised my hand to stop him in his tracks.

"Just go, Damian. Please just leave. There's nothing left to work out."

Damian cursed then slammed the door behind him as he left. I shuffled back to my bedroom, flopped face-forward on my bed and released a batch of tears I had been holding hostage for months. It had been another typical, frustrating episode with Damian Frost.

There was once a time when Damian made me feel like I was the only woman in the world. But when I "cut him off" as he called it, he began to welcome advances from other women and I became less secure in our relationship. I tried to protect my heart by holding back the love and affection I used to give him so freely. He, in turn, did the same, and we were both struggling to make our relationship work when it really wasn't meant to.

When I finally forced myself to get Damian out of my life, I was left alone with my broken spirit and very little faith in love. I felt like a child who had run away from home, and God was waiting there like a father with open arms when I decided to get things right with Him. I vowed that I would never place a man or anything else above my relationship with God because my spirit was too important for me to ignore.

***

I laid on my bed crying so long that I fell asleep and didn't wake up until after ten 'o clock with a headache and hunger pangs. I got up and stretched my tight muscles before I picked up the phone to call Janel.

"Hello?"

"Hey, Girl. It's me," I groaned.

"Hey."

"What are you doing?"

"Nothing. Just watching T.V." she said, sounding hypnotized.

"Let's go eat. I'll pick you up in 15 minutes."

"I don't…"

"Fifteen minutes, Janel," I demanded, and then hung up the phone.

When I arrived at Vanessa and Janel's apartment, I was surprised to see Janel waiting for me on the steps under the glowing street light.

She was wearing a bright sundress, sandals and a frown on her pretty face. She stood to her feet, walked over to the passenger side of the car and let herself in.

"Hey, Girl. Sorry you have to ride in my old-school Altima," I joked. "I would let you drive but I might not make it back home."

Janel gave me a nasty look as she put on her seatbelt.

"Drive," she said unaffected.

I backed out of the parking space and headed to the Waffle House.

"I don't know what your problem is, but this little attitude of yours has got to go. You're a moody little heifer, you know that?"

Janel ignored me. I turned on the radio and drove the rest of the way without saying another word. When we arrived at the restaurant, I turned off the car and unbuckled my seatbelt, but Janel sat motionless. I glanced over at her and saw the moonlight glistening off the tears on her face as she sniffed and wiped her cheeks.

"What's the matter?" I asked, secretly thankful that I hadn't tongue-lashed her the way I really wanted to.

Janel said nothing, but her sobbing became louder. I reached over to her and moved curled strands of hair away from her face.

"Janel, talk to me," I urged.

Her crying became uncontrollable and mascara ran down her face like ink.

"I'm sorry for being a terrible friend to you," she said finally, through sobs.

"You're not a terrible friend, Janel," I said sympathetically.

"Yes I am! I've been a terrible friend to you...and to Vanessa. How could I leave you two stranded like that? It's like I'm bi-polar or something. One minute I'm fine and the next minute I'm doing something stupid. Why did I even go home with him?"

Deep sobs erupted from her throat again.

"With who? What happened?" I asked desperately, fearing the worst.

"He hit me! I told him 'no' and then he hit me. Nobody hits me!" she panicked.

A look of confusion formed on my face, but instead of asking questions, I let her tell the story.

"I'm such a...I can't believe I let myself get into a situation like that!"

She looked out of the window and shook her head before continuing.

"After we left the club, me and this guy...we went to his friend's house. A group of guys were there drinking and playing video games and stuff. After awhile they wanted to play strip poker, so I thought I'd give them a little peep show. But of course they wanted more. They started getting rowdy and cheering for me to take all of my clothes off!"

Janel broke out into sobs again.

I looked at her in amazement. What did she *think* was going to happen while playing strip poker?

"They starting pawing me and pulling off my clothes! One guy forced me on the couch and he...he jumped on top of me. So I bit him, and he slapped me in my face."

"Oh, my God!" I gasped.

"The only reason he didn't rape me was because this other guy grabbed me away from that...that monster and helped me get out of there. They were like wild animals, Destiny. How could I be so stupid?"

I didn't know what to say, so I didn't say anything.

"What if he had raped me, D.? I like sex and all, but I decide when, where and with who? What if he...?"

"But he didn't. He didn't rape you, did he?"

"No, but he could've. I was so scared."

"I guess God sent you an angel last night, even in the midst of all that mess."

"I know," she cried. "The guy who helped me, he drove me home in my car and took a cab back to his place. If it hadn't been for him... God only knows what would've happened."

"Did the guy hurt you? I mean did he leave any marks?" I asked concerned.

"No. I'm okay. I just feel so stupid. And you know what's worse?"

"What?" I asked, appalled that there could be more.

"I don't even remember the name of the guy I followed home," Janel said, sounding ashamed.

Janel and I sat quietly in the car for a few minutes while she cleaned up her face and I digested the awful story she had just told me.

After a deep sigh, Janel said, "You need to find a better friend than me, Destiny."

"Don't get silly on me."

"I mean it. I'm not a good person and I haven't been a good friend to you."

"Shut up, Janel. Let's go inside and eat."

As hungry as I was before, my appetite had dwindled at the thought of something happening to my friend. We went inside, ordered some pancakes and hot chocolate, and ate slowly with very little conversation.

I took the last sip of my hot chocolate before breaking the silence.

"Are you all right?" I asked.

"I guess."

"Are you coming to church tomorrow?"

"I don't know," she said, sounding as if she might cry again. "I don't think God wants to see me right now."

CHAPTER 3

Blessings

The next morning, I was abruptly awakened by the shrill sound of the telephone ringing by my bed.

"Hello?" I said in a groggy voice.

"Wake up, Girl. It's ten-thirty." Vanessa's voice was loud and perky. "I'll be by to pick you up in fifteen minutes."

"Oh, shoot! Okay. I'm getting up."

I hung up the phone and yawned as I crept out of bed. I showered and dressed quickly, and had just enough time to down a piece of toast before Vanessa arrived.

"Hey, Girl!" I said as I plopped onto the front seat of Vanessa's car.

"Hey. Sorry I'm late. I got held up talking to my grandmother."

"If you got here any sooner, Girl, I wouldn't have even been dressed!" I laughed, smoothing my sleeveless floral dress.

Vanessa pulled the car out of the parking space and headed to Victory Temple Christian Church.

"I can't believe this is my last Sunday here," I said nostalgically. "I'm excited about moving, but I'll miss this place, you know? And of course I'll miss you and your crazy self!"

"I know you will!" said Vanessa.

"I guess Janel decided not to come today," I said, half asking a question. In my mind, I recounted how upset she was last night.

"No. I still haven't talked to her. I was out with Rodney all night, and when I got home she wasn't there."

"I know. We went out for a late dinner last night."

Vanessa sucked her teeth. "I don't see how you can just forget about that mess she pulled Friday night."

"She said she was sorry," I said nonchalantly, not wanting to reveal the real reason I forgot about being angry. I wanted to let Janel tell Vanessa about what happened in her own time.

"You'll never guess who came by my place last night," I said, changing the subject.

"Damian?"

"Yeah," I sighed. "I wish I could get him out of my system. It's like I gave him my heart and now he's holding it for ransom. I just want him to give it back to me so I can nurse it back to health and give it to someone who deserves it."

"I know exactly what you mean," said Vanessa as she checked the rear view mirror and changed lanes. "It's like you spend all this time with someone and stir up all these emotions, and for what? Maybe it works out, maybe it doesn't."

"I don't have the strength to do this anymore. I know I need to move on, but the idea of dating other people seems so exhausting. I don't know how some women have relationships with so many men, hoping to find the right one. I don't want to deal with all that. I just want that one person who I can love completely and not feel like I have to hold something back because I might get hurt."

"That day will come," Vanessa said confidently.

"I'm glad you think so. Is it too much to ask for love without the drama? I mean, Damian acts like our relationship is only worthwhile when we're having sex. I thought we had so much more than that. But I guess not." I paused and gazed out of the window. "You know why I think it's so hard for me to let him go?" I asked.

"Because you love him?" guessed Vanessa.

"No. No, I mean I do. I think I do. But...I think it's because I tried to convince myself that he was the one. Now that I know he's not, I wish I could take it all back," I said sadly. "I'm sorry, Girl. I'm sure you're tired of hearing about me and Damian. Let's talk about something else."

"You can talk to me about anything, Destiny. That's what friends are for."

"I'm going to miss having you to talk to, you know?"

"I'll only be a phone call away, D. And I'll come visit you. I might even bring that trifling friend of ours," she said, and we both smiled.

We pulled into the church parking lot twenty minutes after the service started, which meant all eyes were on us as an usher motioned for us to sit down in two cramped seats near the front of the sanctuary. Almost everyone was standing up clapping and singing with the choir. Vanessa and I didn't hesitate to join in. It was one of my favorite songs, and I found myself getting so into the beat that a few club moves slipped out. It felt good, though. I had a lot to be thankful for and I closed my eyes for a few moments to say so.

The pastor spoke his usual hour and ten minutes and closed the sermon saying, "Always remember that God has a plan for your life. There are things that need to be done on this earth that only you can do. And if you are not in place...out of the will of God, you are not in position to receive the blessings He has for you, and others will miss out on the blessing you were meant to be for them."

I became teary-eyed at the pastor's words. It got me thinking about what I really wanted out of life and who I wanted to be. I was a decent person, but not perfect by any means. Dancing at a club on Friday night and dancing in church on Sunday morning isn't exactly saintly. But even with all my shortcomings, God was always blessing me. So, I decided I wanted to be someone who was a blessing to others.

Just before he gave the benediction, Pastor Sanford caught me off guard by calling my name.

"Before we leave today, I want to say a hearty God-bless-you to our sister, Destiny Phillips, as this is her last Sunday with us. Destiny was among the class of graduates from the University of North Carolina, and she will soon be heading to Baltimore to start her career as a photographer."

Pastor Sanford focused his penetrating brown eyes on me and flashed a proud smile.

"Destiny, we know that God will use you in a mighty way," he continued. "And He has already made provisions for you on your new journey. We will be praying for you continually, and although you will be leaving us, you will never leave the presence of God."

A roar of applause filled the sanctuary and the congregation smiled in my direction. I tried to hold them back, but hot tears streamed down my cheeks.

CHAPTER 4

Janel Washington

I was ten years old when my dad came home and found my mom in bed with another man. I heard everything from my bedroom – including the sound of my mom and her lover moaning with pleasure; the sound of the bed banging against the wall; the sound of my dad firing his gun, thankfully missing his target.

The next week when my dad came to pack up his bags, I begged him to take me with him. I even laid on the driveway in front of his car so he wouldn't leave me.

"Janel-Baby," he said to me. "A little girl needs to be with her mother. But you'll always be my little flower. I'll come visit you soon."

I didn't see my dad for another eight years. In those eight years, my mom had many men in her life, though none of them stayed for very long. Some of them were already married; some of them were too young for her; some of them were more interested in me. But I had my fair share of men, too. Some of them were married; some of them were too old for me; some of them were more interested in my mom. I had two abortions by the time I was eighteen.

My dad had the nerve to show up at my high school graduation. He gave me a check for a thousand dollars to get me started in college and told me to call him if I ever needed anything.

When I asked why he never came to see me, he truthfully admitted, "You reminded me too much of your mother."

Most people would consider it a compliment to be likened to their mother. But I tried hard to keep myself from being anything like her, although she was gorgeous, charming and could manipulate people into giving her anything she wanted. She was also extremely vain and always put her needs before mine. A good mother never would've left her 10-year-old daughter alone with a man she hardly knew. I never told my mom he touched me and made me do things I didn't want to do, but I've never forgiven her for leaving me alone with him.

I finally felt free to start a new life when I went to college at UNC to study nursing. No one knew anything about me, so it was the perfect time to change. Unfortunately, some of the bad habits I picked up from my mom never left me.

The only love I've ever known was from the friendship I shared with my two best friends in college, Vanessa and Destiny. They were the only two people who have ever loved me for me. I suppose I could also count the sometimey-love my mom gave me when she wasn't all wrapped up in herself, or the once-every-decade love my dad showed me by giving me gifts. Maybe I could count the temporary physical love I got from the men I let into my bed. There wasn't a man I couldn't have - whenever I wanted him, wherever I wanted him. But the worst thing I've ever done in my life was to prove it.

Last year, my friend Destiny and her boyfriend Damian were having some relationship troubles. It happened at a time when I was feeling especially lonely, so I made a move on Damian and we slept together a few times before he and Destiny got back together. I hated myself for jeopardizing my friendship with Destiny, but Damian promised not to tell, and we went on like nothing happened. The only problem was that I really liked Damian. He was a good guy, and even though he and Destiny had problems, I could tell he really loved her. I wanted someone to love me like that.

I wanted to be loved so badly it hurt. Sometimes I'd sit for hours in my bathroom holding a bottle of pills and wondering if things would be better if I could just go to sleep for a long, long time. Thankfully, it had been awhile since I'd had one of those days. Things weren't perfect, but I found ways to keep myself occupied. I was in my fifth and final year of my nursing program, and I had an internship at a local hospital. I was proud of myself for sticking with it because several times I thought it would be easier to quit and just get a job somewhere. But I really felt like nursing was my calling.

One particular Monday, I had come home from the hospital in an especially foul mood. I had had the worst weekend ever, followed by the worst day at work. My terrible weekend started when I saw Damian at a club trying to get back together with Destiny after they had been broken up for six months. He didn't even say two words to me! Like I didn't even exist! Then later that night, I was at some guy's house that I didn't even know and almost got raped. To top it off, Destiny was there for me when I needed her, just as she always was – which reminded me of how I betrayed her and didn't deserve her friendship. I was starting to hate the person I had become.

I tried to let go of the day and the weekend by taking a long bath and giving myself a manicure. But my mini pampering session was interrupted by the phone ringing.

"Hello?" I said, annoyed at the interruption.

"What's up? It's Damian."

"What do you want?" I snapped.

Damian had been calling me off and on ever since he and Destiny broke up six months ago. All he wanted was to get laid.

"Daaaaang, Woman! What's your problem?"

"You are the one who has a problem? Why are you calling me?"

"Why are you so mad?"

"Because you're a greedy ass bastard!" I cursed. "How can you claim you and Destiny are through when you were all up on her last Friday and didn't say two words to me in the club?"

"Is that what you're all mad about? I was just talking to her, Janel. We're still friends but now she's gone and we're done. So what's up with me and you?"

"Oh! So now that she's gone you want to start paying me some attention!"

I cursed his name a few more times, hung up the phone then threw it on the couch. The nerve of that sorry dog! He was no better than any other man.

Not even an hour later, Damian was knocking on my front door. He knew better than to come to the apartment! If my roommate, Vanessa, found out about me and Damian, it would ruin our friendship. Not to mention my friendship with Destiny.

"What the hell are you doing here?" I snapped, as I flung the door open.

Damian just stood there with his irritatingly sexy smile and said, "You're beautiful when you're mad. Just let me in so we can talk, okay?"

I sucked my teeth and let him come inside. He followed me to my bedroom where I perched myself on my fluffy white bed with my arms folded. Damian sat in my chair, staring at my bare legs hanging out of my shorts.

"Stop looking at me like that," I ordered.

"Why are you so damn mad?" Damian asked, like he had no clue.

"Because I can't stand you," I answered.

"What did I do?"

It felt good that he cared so much about why I was angry. His puppy dog eyes searched my face for some sympathy, but I gave him none.

"All you men care about is sex. If I didn't sleep with you, you wouldn't even be here right now," I said with much attitude.

"That's not true."

"Stop lying," I demanded.

"Listen to me," he said, turning on his charm. "You know I care about you. I just came by to see you, Baby. We don't have to do anything you don't want to."

He let a cunning grin spread across his face, but my expression never changed. I acted like I didn't even hear his stupid remark.

"So, where's Vanessa?" he asked, like the sneaky coward he was.

"She's with Rodney. You know, her man – her man that spends time with her and cares about her even though they don't have sex."

"Is that what this is about? You want me to be your man?" he asked.

"No. I don't want a selfish, cheating man like you. And Destiny shouldn't have put up with your ass either."

"Now you're trying to be a good friend to her, huh?" Damian asked, trying to get smart with me. "You didn't seem to care too much about her when you were in my bed!"

"Don't you dare try to put all the blame on me!" I yelled standing up and pointing a finger in his face. "I wish I'd never slept with you! You weren't worth the risk of losing my friend. Oh, and by the way, Damian," I said in a nasty tone. "The sex isn't all that!"

"Sit down and get your finger out of my face, Janel," he said, angered by my insult.

"You don't tell me what to do in my own house!" I didn't know where all this hatred came from so suddenly, but there was only one person I could direct it toward. I slung more curse words at Damian and flung my arms at him like I would hit him. I felt myself losing control. Suddenly I started pounding away at his chest. Hard.

He grabbed both of my wrists and held them behind my back.

"Let me go!" I screamed.

"All right! Relax!"

I squirmed to get away from him and when I did, I started throwing punches at him again, this time aiming for his face.

"Don't you ever touch me again! I hate you! I hate you!" I shouted.

He grabbed my wrists again and forced me to the bed face first while leaning on me with all his weight.

"Shhh, Janel. I'm not going to hurt you," he said, calming his voice. "Please. Calm down, Baby."

My shouts turned into sobs, and I was a little embarrassed at my outburst. My body gradually went limp, and Damian relaxed his hold on me. I laid there crying for a few minutes while he gently moved hair away from my face and stroked my tear-soaked cheek. Damian must have noticed the pool of snot forming on my bedspread because he went to the bathroom and brought back some tissue for me to wipe my face.

While he was in the bathroom, I sat up on my bed and tried to straighten myself up. What in the world was wrong with me?

"Are you all right?" Damian asked as he sat on the bed next to me and handed me the tissue.

I didn't answer, but took his offering and wiped my nose.

"What was that all about?"

"I'm sorry I hit you," I said weakly. "Maybe you should go." I really didn't want him to go. I just wanted to be consoled. So much crap had been happening to me lately and I wanted someone to make it all go away.

"No, I'll stay," Damian insisted. "I want to make sure you're okay."

"I'm fine," I whispered.

He put his arm around me and I buried my face into his neck like a turtle in a shell. After a few moments, I had calmed myself down and regained my composure. I raised my head from the safety of his neck and stood to my feet, facing Damian and centering myself between his legs.

"You still haven't answered me," he said with such compassion in his voice. "What was all that about? You scared me, Girl."

I delicately placed my hands on his face and planted a loving kiss on each of his eyelids.

"I didn't mean it when I said you were bad in bed, Damian."

"I know," he joked, trying to lighten the mood. He slowly wrapped his arms around my waist. His touch felt soothing and warm. I closed my eyes and pressed my tender lips against his. The kiss tasted bitter sweet, with a slight hint of salty tears.

I released the kiss then asked in a voice as innocent as a child, "Will you hold me? I just need someone to hold me tonight."

"Of course I will," he whispered.

He eased my body onto the bed as he laid next to me. Then I felt his warm mouth placing soft kisses on my face and neck, and I began to cry again. We spent the next hour kissing and embracing with little naps in between.

I felt like I could've stayed in his arms all night in my half-sleep daze. It was the first time in a long time that I felt cared for. But the reality of where I was and who I was with struck me like a sky-fallen piano when I heard, "Oh, my God. Damian, what are you doing here?"

It was Vanessa standing in the doorway of my bedroom. I stirred from my daze and tried to think of something that wouldn't incriminate me in any way. I was thankful we were both fully dressed.

"What are you doing here, Damian?" Vanessa repeated, raising her voice. "You better answer me before I start jumping to conclusions."

"He was just comforting me, Vanessa," I said, like a teenager caught in her bed with a boy.

"I bet he was." Vanessa looked angrier than I've ever seen her. She glared at Damian, then me, shaking her head.

"Destiny hasn't even been gone for one day, and you couldn't wait to come over here for a piece of Janel's tail!" she yelled at Damian. "I always knew you were a dog, but I didn't think you would come sniffing after Destiny's friend!"

Damian stood there silently as Vanessa shifted her attention to me.

"And, Janel, I do use that word 'friend' loosely. How could you do this to Destiny after everything she's done for you? You make me sick to my stomach."

Vanessa turned and went down the short hallway to her bedroom and closed the door.

"I think you should go now," I said to Damian.

As I walked down the hall to Vanessa's room, I realized how much trouble I was in. I couldn't let Destiny find out I had slept with her boyfriend. She would never speak to me again and I needed her in my life. I prayed Vanessa didn't plan to tell Destiny what happened.

I went down the hallway and into Vanessa's bedroom where I was assaulted with the sting of her fury.

"How long have you been sleeping with him, Janel?" Vanessa asked the moment I stepped into her room.

"We didn't do anything! I swear. Just please don't say anything to Destiny. She would never forgive me!"

"You're a liar! How long have you been sleeping with him?"

"Please, Nessa. You and Destiny are the only two people I have

43

in my life who matter to me. It would kill me if she found out about this."

"How long?" Vanessa was almost screaming now. And I started crying again. "Don't give me the water works because it won't get you out of this one."

"It just happened, okay? I didn't mean for things to turn out this way! I swear!" I cried, finally revealing my burning secret.

"I can't believe you! How could you do that to her?"

"I'm sorry! Please don't tell her!" I begged.

"I can't even stand to be around you anymore. You are a self-centered, sorry excuse for a friend. And I'll tell you something else! You've already made a fool out of Destiny and I won't let you do it again. So you better tell her about this or I will. I am not playing with you!"

I started to feel sick. I knew my life would never be the same again.

CHAPTER 5

Easier Said Than Done

My sister, Angel, had a fab-ul-ous two-story condo in a suburb of Baltimore and I couldn't wait to move in with her. She agreed to let me stay with her until I could stand firmly on my own two feet financially, which I hoped wouldn't take too long. I had no bills to pay except gas and groceries, and with my starting salary, I figured I would be ready for my own place in about six months to a year.

Angel was a 27-year-old bachelorette with a great job, a jazzy car and stunning good looks. Most people would think having her 22-year-old sister live with her would cramp her style, but she didn't just see me as her little sister anymore. We had been more like friends ever since my sophomore year in college when she told me I was starting to think more on her level.

After graduating from Howard University, Angel spent the next five years working for a public relations corporation to get as much experience as possible so she could one day open her own firm. Since we were both journalism majors in college, she wanted me to follow in her footsteps so we could start the business together. But my heart had been set on being a photojournalist ever since I was little.

I had been in Baltimore for a week, moving in my belongings

and getting used to the area of town where Angel lived. With less than a week before I began working full-time, I took advantage of every moment to relax and catch up on my daytime television while Angel was at work. I was sitting comfortably on Angel's white leather couch wearing a long t-shirt and watching Oprah when I heard the faint sound of Angel's car pulling into the garage. Her keys jingled as she unlocked the front door and came inside, letting a burst of early-evening sunlight into the living room. She looked sharp in her summer-weight light blue pantsuit with her hair pulled into a smart bun and delicate tendrils framing her face. Her make-up was flawless, and she brought a gentle wave of perfume with her as she placed a handful of mail on the coffee table in front me.

"Hey, Sis."

"Hey, Miss Couch Potato," she said, then kissed me on my forehead. "You've only been here a week and you've already got mail. Somebody must really love you."

"I think it's from Vanessa," I said after I sifted through the pieces of mail and retrieved an envelope addressed to me. It had no return address, but I recognized Vanessa's flowery handwriting. I held the envelope in my lap, deciding I would open it later. "How was your day?" I asked.

"Oh, it was fine," Angel said, kicking off her fancy pumps and heading toward the kitchen. Across the open floor plan, I watched Angel pour herself a glass of iced tea. "I'm telling you, my coworkers can't wait to meet you, Shutterbug. You should stop by my office tomorrow so I can introduce you to everyone. I can take you to lunch after."

"Okay. What time should I be there?" I asked, pleased to have someplace to go.

"Come by at about ten-thirty before everyone leaves for lunch. I'll leave directions for you."

"All right." I said, redirecting my attention to the episode of Oprah.

"What are your plans for the rest of the week?" Angel asked while she removed her suit jacket and draped it across a chair by the kitchen table. She brought her iced tea to the couch with her and sat down on the loveseat.

"I'm trying to avoid leaving the house so I won't spend any money. I have to make the little bit of money I have last until I get my first paycheck."

"I hear that!" Angel said sarcastically. "But seriously, there are things to do here that don't require a lot of money. You can visit the Inner Harbor, go sightseeing in D.C....just get out and meet people."

"Easier said than done. It's no fun going to places like that by myself. But I'm sure I'll meet people here eventually."

"You know, I can help speed up that process if you want. I have a laundry list of people who can't wait to meet my little sister. So just say the word and you have a date!" I could hear the air of excitement in her animated voice. "Mrs. Watson from my church said she has a son about your age and..."

"No, no, no, Angel. I'm not even in the mood to deal with men right now. They're more trouble than they're worth."

"You are way too young to be sounding so bitter. Just because one relationship didn't work out doesn't mean another one won't." Angel took a bobby pin out of her hair and scratched her scalp with it. "Besides, you don't have to fall in love with every man who takes you out. Just have fun, Girl! You're young and beautiful and this city is full of successful brothers looking for someone special to spend some time with. Enjoy yourself."

"Easier said than done," I repeated.

The thought of going on a date repulsed me. It was like begging for the same headaches and heartaches that came when I opened myself up to Damian.

"Maybe I'm not like you, Angel. I don't like to date a bunch of guys who don't mean anything to me." As soon as I said it, I regretted the way it came out.

"And what's that supposed to mean?" Angel asked.

"I didn't mean to say it like that. I mean...don't you get tired of dating?"

"No, I don't," she answered calmly. "Let me tell you something, Shutter. I know you have these high hopes of Prince Charming knocking on your door and sweeping you off your feet. But what happens if that day doesn't come for another ten years? Are you going to hibernate and twiddle your thumbs until that great day arrives? I should think not. What you have to do is enjoy life day to day. You of all people know that each new day is not promised to you. So don't sit around waiting for Mr. Perfect. There's nothing wrong with making new friends and enjoying people's company. The world is much bigger than UNC and your little circle of friends, so come out and join it."

"I know. You're right," I sighed. "I just get so discouraged sometimes. I feel like I'll never meet a man who is everything I need him to be. Maybe I'm too picky."

"You're not too picky. You just have standards. High ones, like me. I know how you feel, okay. I've been out here for much longer than you and I understand your frustration. But being bitter about it is only going to rob you of happiness in the meantime. Don't be afraid of love or you won't even recognize it when it finds you."

Angel stood to her feet and took her perspiring glass of ice back to the kitchen. "Dinner's on you tonight," she said. "I'm going to take a shower and get comfortable."

As soon as Angel disappeared upstairs, I retreated to my room with my thoughts and the envelope I got in the mail. I flipped up the light switch, and then ran a tear through the back of the envelope with my thumb. Standing in the middle of the room, I pulled out a greeting card and read the formal message before taking in the words Vanessa had hand-written on the left-side of the card.

"I miss you, D.," the letter read. "You're the best friend a girl could have and I couldn't be happier for you. Congrats on your new job. I know God has special plans for your life. Your best friend, Vanessa."

"I miss you, too, Lady." I whispered, as I displayed the card on my nightstand.

I thought about calling Vanessa to thank her for thinking of me. I was missing her, too; but I was feeling a little down after my conversation with Angel and I didn't want her to think things weren't going well. Things were great actually. But I couldn't get Angel's words out of my head. *Don't be afraid of love or you won't even recognize it when it finds you.*

I began to wonder if real love would ever find me, or if it already had. I tried to shake away thoughts of Damian; how much I had loved him and how much I had already sacrificed for our relationship. Was it all in vain? Was he a waste of time, love and tears? Even with all my unanswered questions, I had to admit to myself that I wanted him there with me. I wanted someone familiar to share my new city and help me explore all there was to do and see.

In a rare moment of weakness, I decided I needed to talk to Damian. Just for a second. I rushed back into the living room to pick up the cordless phone resting on the end table. I brought the phone back to my room, closed my door and sat on the plush, carpeted floor with my back against my bed.

I dialed Damian's cell phone number, and after four rings, I heard his voice on the other end.

"Hello?"

"Hey, Damian. It's me."

"What's up, Baby? I've been thinking about you." Damian sounded strangely pleased to hear from me.

"You don't even know who this is, do you?"

"Don't even try it, Girl. This is the woman who broke my heart and left me here to rot while she ran off to Baltimore to take over the world," he joked.

"Lucky guess. How have you been?"

"I'm better now that you called. You didn't even leave me your number or else I would've tried to call you."

"Yeah?"

"Yeah. So, how have *you* been?" he asked.

"I'm doing fine. Great."

"How's the job treating you?"

"I don't start until Monday. I'm just kinda hangin' out right now."

"Cool. Give me a call and let me know how your first day at work goes. I wanna hear all about your exciting new career, Miss Photojournalist," he charmed.

"Okay."

I paused and tried to lighten the tone of my voice. Damian always accused me of being too serious.

"You know," I said. "I wanted to apologize for the way I left things between us. That night at my apartment…I don't want our argument to be your last memory of me."

"I can think of better ways to say goodbye."

"I know."

"So what do we do now?" he asked.

"What do you mean?"

"I mean, where do we go from here? I still love you, Baby. I'm willing to try to work things out - even with the long distance between us."

"I don't know if that's such a great idea."

"Why not?"

"Because there's nothing else left to work out," I said sadly, as I traced imaginary shapes into the carpet. "That's why we broke up six months ago. We've tried and tried and it's obvious that we weren't meant to be together."

"Don't say that. I know we can make it work this time," he said, convinced.

"What makes you think things will be better this time?"

"Because, I'll do whatever it takes. I don't want to be with anyone else but you."

"I thought you said you weren't ready to settle down yet."

"I changed my mind," he said. "I've been doing a lot of thinking lately, and I realized that I don't need to look any further for the perfect woman because I've already found her."

"Well, that may be fine for you, but I'm not sure I'm ready to do this with you again. I just don't think we're good for each other. All we do is fight and say things to hurt each other. Love shouldn't be this hard."

"Who said love is supposed to be easy?" he asked.

"I know it won't always be easy, but it shouldn't be like this." I sighed. "I need to be with someone who believes the same things I do and is working toward the same goal as mine."

"You know I believe in God and all that," he said, sounding mildly insulted.

"I never said you didn't. I just want more. I want it to feel right, and it doesn't."

"Whatever problems we have we can fix them if we really want to."

"I don't think so, Damian. I think we should accept the fact that we're just not right for one another."

"Then what did you call me for, huh? Just to throw it in my face that you're ready to move on without me?" he barked.

"You know me better than that. But if you don't want to talk to me, I'm sorry I called. I guess I'll let you go."

"No, Baby, don't hang up. I didn't mean to say that."

"No, you're right. I shouldn't have called you."

"Wait! I'm sorry. Don't hang up. Listen to me," he begged. "There's a reason you called me tonight, Destiny. Because you still love me and somewhere deep down you know that there's still something between us. I'm willing to give you your space while you figure out what you really want. But just know that I'll be here whenever you make up your mind."

"You know," I said softly. "Sometimes I wish I had never fallen in love with you."

"I'm glad you did, Baby. I love you so much, but I'm so sick of fighting with you all the time."

"Me, too," I said.

"Then let's stop fighting. Let's work this thing out."

When we got off the phone, a steady trail of familiar tears streamed down my face. *When am I going to stop doing this to myself*, I wondered. It was so apparent that Damian was no good for me, but I kept going back for more. Our relationship was toxic. It drained me of energy and joy, but I couldn't bring myself to let him go.

CHAPTER 6

Find A New One

The next day, a Friday, I decided to put Damian out of my mind and enjoy my new freedom. I had plans to have lunch with Angel and do a little window shopping, so I took extra care getting dressed. I selected a flattering skirt, a sleeveless blouse, and high-heeled, strappy sandals to wear for the occasion. I spent a half-hour curling my hair, and though I wasn't much for make-up, I felt I might need some today, just to perk me up. It was really the first time I had anywhere to go since I'd been in town, and I was ready to face the city head on.

Angel always gave great directions, so I didn't have any trouble finding the PR firm where she worked called Grant & Elliott Media Group. When I arrived at the stately building, I entered through the large glass doors and approached a middle-aged white woman sitting at the reception desk. She had a round, friendly face with glasses, and curly brown hair pulled away from her forehead.

"How may I help you, ma'am?" she asked.

"Hi. I'm here to see Angel Phillips. I'm her sister."

"Sure. I'll let her know you're here."

The woman, whose nameplate read "Anna Washburn," picked up the phone then punched a few numbers. "Ms. Phillips, your sister is waiting for you in the lobby," she said.

As I waited for Angel, I let my eyes roam the tasteful décor and walls adorned with numerous company plaques and awards. A few minutes later I saw my beautiful sister emerge from a corridor to the left of the reception desk, holding a short stack of folders to her chest. She was wearing a plum-colored, short-sleeved dress with a cheerful scarf tied at the side of her neck. Her hair was pulled into an up-do, which brought attention to her gorgeous African-style earrings.

"Hey, Shutterbug!" Angel came toward me and gave me a one-armed hug. "I'm glad you found the place okay. Let me introduce you to Anna, our secretary. Anna, this is my sister, Destiny. I'm sure you've already met."

"Good to meet you officially, Anna."

"Nice to meet you, too, Shutterbug," Anna said jokingly as we shook hands.

"See, Angel, I told you not to call me that in public."

Angel ignored me and said, "Destiny is a photographer for the *Baltimore Sun*."

"How wonderful!" Anna exclaimed. "I'll have to look for your photos in tomorrow's paper."

"Oh, I haven't started working yet, but I should have something in there sometime next week."

"I'll keep my eyes open," Anna said with a little wink.

As Angel guided me through the building, she introduced me to a series of suit-clad executives and friendly PR specialists before we finally got to her office. Angel's office was small, but it was hers, and she had added her own special touches to personalize it. She even had a picture of the two of us taken on the day she graduated from college.

We chatted for a few minutes as she caught me up on some of her clients and how she was trying to handle her load while conducting research about starting her own firm. She had been looking for a location for her business, but was understandably apprehensive about jumping out on her own, although she was well-qualified.

At about 11:30, we headed to an Italian restaurant not far from Angel's office. I ordered a sampling of spaghetti, lasagna and fettuccini alfredo, while Angel had chicken parmesan. As we waited for our lunch, we snacked on bread dipped in olive oil and Angel continued her interrogation from last night.

"So, have you thought about what we talked about last night?"

"Thought about what?" I asked with a playful smirk. I knew what she meant. Angel shot me her famous "Don't play with me" look. "Yeah, I thought about it a little bit. But it led me into doing something stupid."

"What?"

"I called Damian."

"Why?"

"I don't know, but I wish I hadn't. I felt terrible afterward. He said he wants us to try to work it out."

"Is that what you want?" Angel asked.

"I don't know."

"Look, Shutter. Forget about what he wants. You just need to decide if you want him in your life or not."

"I don't want him. We haven't been a couple for almost six months. But there's just something inside of me that doesn't want to let him go."

"Well, you know what they say. The quickest way to get over a man is to find a new one. Now, I told you about Mrs. Watson's son. I bet he's cute because Mrs. Watson is a pretty lady and her husband is…"

"Angel!"

"Just listen! I'll call her tonight and tell her to bring him to church on Sunday. Then you can meet him and decide if you want to go on a date with him."

"What makes you think he would want to go out with me?"

"Oh, please! You are my sister, and good genes run in the family!" she sassed.

I laughed at her as I moved my hands away from the table so the waiter could place my salad bowl in front of me.

"Would you like crushed pepper on your salad?" ask the waiter.

"No, thank you," Angel said. When the waiter left, Angel distributed salad into her bowl and mine.

"All right. I'll meet this Watson boy," I said. "But don't make it seem like I'm pressed."

"I got your back, Baby Sister."

We laughed and talked and joked through lunch then Angel had to get back to work. She gave me directions to an outlet mall just south of Baltimore on I-95. I wanted to do some window shopping and add a new location to my knowledge base.

I easily found the outlet mall and parked in front of my favorite discount store. I spent the next hour browsing through the jumbled assortment of clothing, shoes, purses and jewelry before I ventured into the rest of the mall. Before attacking the other stores, I needed to quench my parched throat, so I went to the food court to get a drink. I went to a fast food restaurant and waited in line behind an elderly couple placing an order.

I suddenly felt a pair of eyes burning a hole in the back of my head. Using my peripheral vision, I spotted a tall, brown-skinned man who looked to be in his late twenties, early thirties. He was flat out gawking at me, wearing loose khakis and an un-tucked, iron-crisp shirt with a clean, white t-shirt underneath. He had just finished tossing a soft drink cup in the trash can and stood there as if his feet were glued to the ground.

Oh, Lord, I thought to myself. *Please don't let him be a bugaboo. What kind of man is at the mall at two-thirty in the afternoon? Doesn't he have a job or something? Why is he staring like that? Doesn't he know that's rude?*

I let out an annoyed sigh and stepped forward to order some lemonade. And just as I'd feared, the man began walking toward me once I picked up my drink.

"Excuse me, Miss. Can I talk to you for a second?"

"Sure," I said dryly as he approached me in the middle of the food court.

"I'm sorry to bother you, but you look familiar."

Did he really just say that?

"No, I don't think we've met before." I took a sip of my lemonade and let my eyes leisurely examine this bold brother. Standing at about six feet, I noticed he was somewhat attractive, and wore a blanket of worldly wisdom on his face. He won a few extra brownie points with his precision-cut goatee, a shiny bald head and straight teeth. Smelled pretty good, too.

"Where are you from? Because you look like a girl I knew back home in L.A."

"I'm definitely not from L.A. I've never even been there before." I hoped I wasn't sounding too annoyed, but I was.

"Well you should definitely visit some time. It's the spot." He paused for a moment and looked me dead in my eyes. "I'm Terrance, by the way."

"My name is Destiny."

"I hope you don't mind me saying so, Destiny, but you are an extremely attractive woman."

"Thank you," I said, unwilling to return the compliment.

"Care to join me?" he asked, taking a seat at a nearby table.

It wasn't my usual policy to sit down and chat with a total stranger on request, but I really had nothing else better to do. I reluctantly sat across from him and responded to his numerous queries. What do you do? Where are you from? Where did you go to school? Do you have a man?

I, in turn, learned that Terrance lived in Los Angeles and was in town for his cousin's wedding. He was a self-employed publicist who worked with low-level entertainers and the occasional low-budget movie star. I told him my sister was also in public relations, which spun our conversation into yet another direction.

After about fifteen minutes, my irritation from this meeting of a stranger subsided, and I actually began to enjoy talking to Terrance.

"You're all right, Destiny. I could really hang out with you," he said, his stare forcing me to look him in the eye. "I know you hardly know me and I'm only in town for the weekend, but I'd like to take you out tomorrow night. I promise to be good company."

"Don't you have to spend time with your family after the wedding?" I asked.

"Naw, the wedding is pretty early. I'll be done with everything by five or six. I'll pick you up at eight, okay?"

I shook my head and pursed my lips as I thought about how fine this brother must've thought he was. He wore confidence like an Armani suit, which reminded me a little too much of Damian.

"You seem like someone who's used to getting what he wants," I stated. Terrance smiled and shrugged his shoulders as if to say "I got it like that!"

Although I didn't feel ready to start dating again, I had taken Angel's words to heart. *Don't be afraid of love or you won't even recognize it when it finds you.* I was almost positive this wasn't love. But it would be a start. It could be just what I needed to get Damian out of my mind and maybe one day, out of my heart.

I told Terrance I would meet him at the hotel where he was staying at 8 p.m. Saturday. We exchanged phone numbers before he dashed off to the airport to pick up a relative who was flying in town for the wedding.

When I got home and told Angel I had a date, she nearly peed on herself.

CHAPTER 7

Waiting to be Adopted

"Now, I want you to go on this date with an open mind," Angel commanded, as she ran the comb through my hair. "Remember, all you have to do is have fun. Don't worry about if this is the man you're supposed to marry. Don't start comparing him to past boyfriends and please don't focus on his flaws all evening. The worst that can happen is that you get a free meal. And who knows? Maybe you'll make a new friend. But your only job tonight is to have a good time, all right?"

"Yes, ma'am," I said sarcastically. Angel loved giving advice and I was in no position to reject it. So I didn't. I let her finish curling and twirling my hair, then I dressed for my date with Terrance.

Just have fun. I can do that, I thought to myself as I carefully situated myself into my car. My nails were still a little wet from the fresh manicure Angel gave me.

I drove about ten miles to the fancy hotel where Terrance told me he was staying. He gave me his room number, but I didn't feel comfortable going there on a first date. So, I asked the clerk at the front desk to call him for me.

"I'm sorry, ma'am. No one is picking up the call. Are you sure you have the right room?"

"I think so," I said. "I'll just try a cell phone number. May I use your phone?"

"Sure, as long as it's a local call."

I sifted through my purse and found the receipt where I had written down Terrance's room and cell phone number. His cell phone had a Los Angeles area code.

"Oh, it's long-distance. Is there a pay phone I can use?" It was times like these when I wished I had a cell phone myself. It just happened to be a bill I couldn't afford at the time.

"You can use my cell phone if you're only going to be a minute," said a lady checking in next to me with another clerk.

"Oh, thank you!" I exclaimed. "I'll just be a second."

I was a little ticked that Terrance wasn't in his room, but I gave him the benefit of the doubt and considered he might've gotten into an accident or something.

When I dialed Terrance's number, I heard an unfamiliar voice on the other end of the line.

"Can I speak to Terrance please?"

"He's a little busy right now. Can I take a message?"

"Yes, please tell him that Destiny is on the phone. We were supposed to be going on a date tonight at eight."

"Destiny, huh? You've got a sexy voice, Destiny. Hold on a minute."

"Hello?" said a voice I faintly recognized as Terrance's.

"Did you forget about our date tonight?" I asked.

"My date with Destiny. How could I forget?"

"Well, you must've forgotten that you were supposed to meet me at your hotel at eight."

"Oh! Is it eight already? I'm so sorry, I just got caught up at the reception and all. I'll be over there in twenty minutes, okay?"

"No, it's not okay! I don't even know you and you expect me to wait around for you like a groupie! Forget the date. Have a safe trip back to L.A."

I hit the 'end' button on the cell phone then thanked the nice lady who let me borrow it.

I couldn't believe the audacity Terrance had in asking me to wait for him after he had forgotten about our date. Maybe if he was a friend of mine it wouldn't have bothered me as much. But it already took everything in me just to accept his date - then he had the nerve to pull this!

I got in my car, all dressed up with no place to go. So I went home. Angel was more disappointed by the incident with Terrance than I was. I ended up going to a jazz club with Angel and a few of her girlfriends that night. Even though I didn't get a free meal, I actually had a good time.

***

Though we were tired from our evening out on the town, Angel and I woke up on Sunday in time to make it to church. She made a special effort to be there today because she was hoping Mrs. Watson would bring her son for me to meet. I couldn't have cared less because my luck with men had obviously run out. I was still disgusted at Terrance and I didn't even know him.

The church Angel frequented was a rather large African-Methodist Episcopal church about twenty minutes away from the condo. The parking lot looked like a car show with shiny, expensive SUVs and luxury vehicles filling every space. A few other late-comers strolled in as we approached the building, dressed in impeccable suits and stylish dresses and hats. I felt underdressed, even in my Sunday best.

"How did you find this place?" I asked Angel, as our Sunday heels click-clacked up to the front door of the church.

"Kamira told me about it. Her family has gone here for years. The congregation is a little stiff, but the Word and the music are pretty good. You'll see."

Angel was right. Stiff was the word. We found seats in the balcony and were able to see everything and everyone in the church, so neat, proper and perfectly placed.

The music was wonderful, though. The congregation stood up and sang along with the choir that was dressed in lily white robes. As prim and proper as everyone seemed, I almost forgot that it was okay to close my eyes, worship and get into the service. Without my permission, a single tear leaked from my eye as the words to the song touched my spirit. I felt at peace because God knew. Of all the tragic things that go on in the world, and all the crises people face everyday, God knew my every worry and pain, no matter how insignificant it may seem to anyone else.

I sometimes felt guilty praying for myself because there were so many other people who needed God's attention more than I did. I was blessed. I was healthy. I was relatively successful in everything I set out to do. I had a loving family, great friends, and wonderful opportunities to explore all that life had to offer. Why should I come crying to God just because I was a little sad over breaking up with some guy? It seemed so unimportant in the grand scheme of life. But God told me a long time ago that He knows and He cares, and everything that happened to me was important to Him.

The choir sang an array of soul-stirring songs, followed by church announcements, collection of tithes and offerings, and the sermon. After church, Angel and I waited in front of the building for her friend Kamira and her family, but I knew they weren't the only ones we were waiting for.

"Mrs. Watson!" Angel called in the direction of a heavy-set woman with a beautiful round face wearing a royal purple dress.

"Hello, Miss Angel! It's good to see you!"

Mrs. Watson engulfed Angel's slim frame with a deep, hearty hug.

"Let me introduce you to my sister, Destiny."

Angel stretched one of her arms out to me.

"Hello, Mrs. Watson, I've heard a lot about you," I said, bracing myself for Mrs. Watson's hug.

Her wide body was soft and cozy like a mama bear, and her floral-scented perfume was pleasant to the nose. I was amazed at the smoothness of her milk chocolate skin and how bright and captivating her smile was. She looked as if she could be a plus-sized model.

"I've heard much about you, Miss Destiny! Aren't you a beautiful sight! Both of you are just beautiful."

I smiled and fidgeted with the shoulder strap on my purse.

"So, was your son able to make it?" asked Angel, sounding terribly forward and desperate on my behalf.

"No, My Dear, Jonathon has a business meeting tomorrow in Atlanta, so he's catching a flight as we speak. He would've loved to meet you, though, Destiny. He's always talking about how it's hard to find good women these days. But I'll make sure he makes it to church next time he's home."

I was grateful that Mrs. Watson's son, I guess Jonathon was his name, wasn't able to make it. Between his mother and my sister, I felt like an orphan waiting to be adopted by the first man willing to take me in.

After exchanging a few pleasantries with some of Angel's church acquaintances, we headed back to the condo and made some sandwiches for lunch. Angel wanted to have brunch with Kamira and her family, but I told her I wanted to wash my car and get myself physically and mentally prepared for my first day of work.

CHAPTER 8

A Bona Fide Photojournalist

I welcomed Monday morning like an oasis in the desert. I was ready to start working and get my mind focused on something productive besides talk shows and Lifetime T.V. I rose bright and early so I could leisurely get dressed in the new pant suit my mother helped me pick out before I left for Baltimore, eat breakfast and get to work in my freshly-washed Altima without worrying about traffic.

The *Baltimore Sun* was Maryland's largest newspaper, with its only competition being the Washington Post. Usually, the paper only hired photojournalists with at least three to five years experience shooting for a daily newspaper. But my summer internships in North Carolina helped me land my job straight out of college. John Mitchell, the director of photography, was my new boss. He was a pretty friendly guy, shorter-than-average in height with a striking resemblance to Edward Norton from the movie Fight Club.

When I arrived at the office, John introduced me to the other 18 photographers on staff, then a lady named Gloria helped me fill out my W-4 and other employment paperwork. At 9 a.m., I attended my first daily assignment meeting as a bona fide photojournalist with a steady paycheck. John had even added my name to the photo assignments board on the wall.

My first assignment of the day was pretty tame at best. I was sent out with a young reporter named Jesse Newburn to cover the grand opening of a new restaurant in downtown Baltimore. It must've been THE day for grand openings because not long after we returned to the office, I was sent back out to cover the grand opening of a new art museum.

It wasn't the most fast-paced, action-packed day in the life of a photographer, but it was work, and I was happy doing it. When I got home that night, I unloaded all the details of my day onto Angel who listened with as much enthusiasm as she always had - an abundance. I also called my mom and daddy in Richmond and told them all about my first day of employment.

"Hello, my little Shutterbug!" my mother said when she answered the phone.

"Hey, Mama!"

"How was your first day at work?"

"It was good. I covered the grand openings of a new restaurant and an art museum. I guess a fire or a gang shootout would've opened up the opportunity for more interesting photos, but I'll take what I can get right now."

"That's wonderful! I'm so proud of you, Sweetheart. You and your sister are so amazing."

"We haven't done anything amazing, Mama."

"Yes, you have. You two have grown up to be beautiful, God-fearing women who have the strength and the courage to reach whatever goals you set for yourselves. I call that amazing."

"Well, we're only amazing because of you and daddy."

"You're amazing because God made you that way."

"If you say so."

"How's your living arrangement working out? You two haven't gotten into any squabbles have you?"

"No, ma'am. I actually like living with Angel. We're getting along really well."

"That's good. That's great. Is your car holding up all right?"

"Yes, ma'am."

"Good. Good. How's Damian?"

I just knew she was going to ask about him! I didn't know how I felt about him at the moment, so I didn't know what to tell her.

"He's fine."

"Are you two still an item?"

"I don't know, Mama. I'm a little confused about Damian right now."

"Well, Shutterbug, you know God is not the God of confusion. If there is anything you want or need to know, ask Him, and He'll tell you."

"I will." I cleared my throat. "Where's Daddy?"

"He's right here. I'll get him for you. Give Angel my love."

"Okay."

A few moments later, it sounded as if Barry White had picked up the phone, but the voice on the other end was James Phillips, my daddy.

"How's it going, Shutter?" he asked.

"I'm good, Daddy. I had my first assignments today."

"What did you shoot?"

"Nothing too exciting. Just photos of a new restaurant and an art museum."

"That's good, Baby Girl. I'm proud of you. You're doing what you always wanted to do, and that's all we ever wanted for you and your sister."

It may sound corny, but I truly loved and admired my parents. I'm aware that stories are more interesting when they're about tragic childhoods and deadbeat parents. But believe it or not, James and Lena Phillips actually made it work. Thanks to their successful careers as real estate agents, my parents were able to raise their daughters in an upper-middle class side of Richmond, providing us the best of everything, from private elementary schools to family vacations to Jamaica almost every year.

My mother was a borderline saint. My father was strong and loving, but over-protective at times. I hated it as a kid, but as I looked back on my life, I realized that I really didn't miss out on much. I remember a conversation I had with Vanessa and Janel one night when we lived in the dorms. We were talking about qualities we were looking for in a man, and the more I thought about it, the more I realized that I wanted a man with the same qualities that my dad naturally possessed. He was intelligent, proud, God-fearing, attentive to my mother, and had a smile that could light up a room. My dad was my only proof that good men really do exist. Maybe he was why I was so picky.

I was destined to be on the phone all night after my call home. I still had two other people I couldn't wait to share my day with. I even tossed around the idea of trying to reach Damian.

I called Vanessa and Janel's apartment, but no one was home, so I left a message on their answering machine then called Janel on her cell phone.

"Hello?" she answered.

"Nelly Nel! What's going on, Girl!" I shouted, excited that I had reached her.

"Destiny? Wow. How have you been?"

"I'm good. Today was my first day at work."

"Really? How was it?" Janel asked dispassionately.

"It was good." I was somewhat disappointed at my friend's lack of excitement about hearing from me for the first time in almost two weeks.

"How are things with you?"

"I'm fine. Just working at the clinic part-time and going to school."

"I called the apartment, but Vanessa wasn't home. How has she been? I miss you guys."

"Vanessa's fine," Janel said, sounding distant. "Let me take down your phone number. I'll tell her to call you."

I gave Janel my number, and then she gave me a weak excuse for why she had to get off the phone with me.

I hung up the phone feeling a little hurt. Had Janel decided that since I didn't live near her she didn't need me as a friend anymore? The thought bothered me, so I decided to call her back.

"Janel, it's me again," I said when she picked up the phone. "What's going on?"

"What do you mean?"

"Come on. I know you. I know when something's not right. How are things at home?"

"Everything is fine, Destiny, I'm just really busy. I promise I'll call you soon, okay? I'll tell Vanessa to call you."

I still wasn't satisfied. But I couldn't make her talk if she didn't want to.

"All right," I relented. "Call me soon."

Something just didn't sit right with me after talking to Janel. But I let it go for the moment.

I spent another hour on the phone when Vanessa called me at ten o'clock that evening. It was satisfying to share my day and my new experiences with a friend who was genuinely excited for me. I was just as excited to hear that Vanessa had already gotten a promotion on her job.

"Oh, and guess what else, Girl," she added.

"What?"

"Rodney proposed to me last night!"

"Get outta here! I knew it was coming soon. How did he do it?"

"On one knee in the park where we had our first kiss!"

"Nessa, that is so sweet! I'm gonna have to give Rodney props for that one. I bet the ring is niiiiice."

"I'll show it to you in a couple of weeks."

"What are you talking about?" I asked with a suspicious smile.

"I'm coming to see you. In two weeks. Rodney has to go out of town that weekend, so I figured it would be a good time to check out my girl in B-more."

"You have just made my week! Is Janel coming, too?"

"I don't know what's going on with that girl. I haven't spoken to her since you left."

"That doesn't make sense, Nessa. You two live together."

"Well, that doesn't mean I have to like her."

"What did she do now? I spoke to her today and she was acting kinda funny."

"I don't want to talk about her anymore. But your answer is 'no'. Janel is not coming with me."

I decided not to push the issue with Vanessa. I was just ecstatic that she was coming to see me.

***

During the next few weeks, I channeled all my energy toward my photography and learning everything I could about the industry. The more I worked, the more confident I became in my talent, and my portfolio was filling up fast. Angel, with her entrepreneurial mind, told me I should get a small business license, some fancy business cards, and a bold-face phone listing in the upcoming Yellow Pages for my own photography service. The business would be called *Destiny's Images* – a name I had dreamed up when I first discovered my love for photography at the tender age of 12. I told Angel that the business was a great idea, but it would have to wait. It would be too difficult to commit to clientele when I was on-call at the *Sun* most nights and weekends. Nevertheless, I was enthusiastic about what I was doing, and the opportunities were boundless.

My focus on work was intermittently distracted by calls from Damian. I'll admit that I enjoyed hearing from him. I found it unnerving that he paid more attention to me now that I was in Baltimore than he did when I lived ten minutes away from him. He ended every phone call with an "I love you." And he had mentioned several times that he was making plans to come visit me. I just listened to him talk mostly. I hadn't revealed to him that I still had strong feelings for him, and my distrust of my slick-talking ex-boyfriend was starting to soften.

I still hadn't heard from Janel, and every time I asked Vanessa about her she would change the subject. I just left it alone. I figured if Janel wanted to continue our friendship, she would call me when she was ready.

CHAPTER 9

Is This What I Get?

It was a Friday evening in late August when Vanessa showed up at my door looking as bright and sunny and as the day had been. Her smile revitalized me like a breath of fresh air.

"Hey, Girl!"

"Heeeey!" I shouted as Vanessa stepped through the doorway and into my embrace. I hugged her tightly. "I missed you! How was the drive up here? You must've run right into traffic."

I released her and took a bag off of her shoulder.

"Yeah, I thought I left early enough to avoid the rush, but I guess not."

"Let me see that rock!" I demanded before Vanessa stepped one more foot into the condo. She daintily displayed the shimmering princess-cut diamond with a platinum band wrapped around her finger. "You go, Rodney! This ring is beautiful. I'm so happy for you, Girl." I hugged her again.

Vanessa surveyed the condo. "This place is gorgeous! You and Angel are living it up!"

"I guess. This is her place, though. I'm just freeloading until I get on my feet. Come on. I'll show you my room."

I got Vanessa settled then we sprawled across my bed and gabbed.

"Tell me about the wedding plans?"

"We've set a date for July 20th of next year. My mother insists that it takes a year to plan a wedding. I really don't care when we have it. I'm just glad to have Rodney."

"He's a lucky man."

"I know," Vanessa said boastfully.

"How are things going with Sisters on the Rise?"

"Good. Things are moving in the right direction. We just finished the new curriculum for the girls ages 14-18. We added tips for studying effectively, and we just recruited a new instructor to teach a course in how to manage finances."

"I'm so proud of you, Nessa. It must feel great to know that what you do everyday directly impacts the community. I would love to be a part of something like that."

"You'd be surprised at the opportunities there are to help young girls around here. You don't have to do it full time to make a difference."

"Yeah. I guess I need to look into that."

"Enough about my life. What have you been up to lately? Any more phantom dates?"

I laughed at the recollection of my non-existent date with Terrance. "No, I think I'm done with the dating scene for awhile," I said.

"What? I know you haven't given up that easy."

"It's not that I've given up. It's more like I've given in. I'm thinking about trying it with Damian one more time."

"I thought you two have been through for months now."

"We had been, but I told you he's been calling and we've sorted some things out. I really miss him and I don't want to risk losing him by expecting too much."

"Expecting too much? Where is all this coming from? You told me that he didn't give you what you needed – spiritually or emotionally. When did all of that change?"

"I don't know, but it has," I said, getting a little defensive. "I just want to make sure our relationship has no unfinished business. I'll never be able to get over him unless I know there's no future for us."

"Destiny, you won't ever get over him until you let him go. He's not good for you. You told me that yourself. I've listened to you whine about him and go back and forth about your feelings for him. I thought by moving to Baltimore, you would be ready for a fresh start."

"Why are you so against me getting back together with Damian?"

"Why are you so set on taking him back?"

"Whatever. Let's talk about something else."

"Fine with me," Vanessa said, sounding relieved to end the conversation.

Vanessa's conviction regarding my relationship with Damian was shocking. I didn't know where all this sudden hatred for him came from, but I didn't want to spend Vanessa's first night in Baltimore arguing, so I let it go.

Angel came home later that night, and the three of us went out for dinner. We talked about anything and everything except my relationship with Damian.

Vanessa and I spent the next day shopping and eating, with more shopping and eating in between. And that night, we decided to join Angel and her friends Kamira and Janet for a night out on the town. For a change of scenery, we drove about an hour to Washington, D.C. and went dancing at a popular nightclub in the heart of the district.

We got home from the club around three o'clock in the morning, and while Vanessa took a shower in my bathroom, I checked my voicemail.

"First message. Yesterday. Ten-thirty-six p.m." said the automated voicemail lady.

"Hey, Baby. It's me. I just wanted to see how your day was. Call me when you get this. I love you. Oh, don't make plans for this weekend. I have a surprise for you." The voice on the message belonged to Damian.

"End of message. To replay this message, press 1. To save this message, press two. To delete this message, press three." I pressed two. "Next message. Yesterday. Eight-seventeen p.m."

"Destiny, this is John. I'm going to need you to work the late shift Monday, so don't plan to come in until two. Call me to let me know you received this message. Have a great weekend!" said John in a cheerful voice.

Perfect. Extended weekend, I thought to myself. As I deleted the message, I debated whether or not I should call Damian while Vanessa was there. I felt insecure about my decision to reconnect with him ever since I told Vanessa about it. Her opinion had always meant a lot to me, and her doubts made me doubt.

I decided to wait until Vanessa left before calling Damian. That would give me more time to figure out how I really felt about him.

***

I felt like somewhat of a heathen Sunday morning when I woke up at 11:57 a.m. Vanessa and I laid around the condo all day talking, eating and watching T.V. instead of going to church. We were lying on the couch in our pajamas watching re-runs of the Cosby Show when I asked Vanessa a question I had been waiting to pose ever since she came to town.

"What's going on between you and Janel?" I asked.

"Destiny, please. I told you I don't want to talk about her."

"Best friends talk about everything, Vanessa. And you two have been mad at each other for over a month now. She's not even talking to me. So if you know why, I'd appreciate it if you would tell me."

Vanessa sighed and shook her head. "This is so messed up."

"What?"

"She's not even woman enough to tell you herself."

Vanessa paused, turned around and looked toward the staircase as if she were looking for Angel to come downstairs from her bedroom.

"What is it, Nessa?"

"You're never going to forgive me after I tell you this, but it's not fair for you to be in the dark."

"Just spit it out. Is Janel sick or something?"

"No. It's just hard for me to be the one to tell you."

"Tell me what?" All the secrecy was starting to tick me off.

"Janel is not the friend you think she is."

"Keep talking," I encouraged.

Vanessa took a deep breath and looked me in my eyes. "Janel and Damian slept together. I told her if she didn't tell you then I would have to."

Vanessa might as well have shot me in my face. A rush of hot pain flooded my head.

"What did you say?" I asked in disbelief.

"I'm so sorry, D. You have to know that I didn't want to be the one to tell you something so hurtful. But neither of those two cowards planned to tell you the truth."

"Wait. How? When did you find out about this? Did Janel tell you she did that?"

"I saw them in her bedroom the day you left UNC. Janel admitted to me that they had slept together before."

My heart felt like an anvil. As Vanessa spoke the most evil words I had ever heard, my mind swirled with unanswered questions, and my body felt as if it would collapse.

"Please tell me you're joking. Vanessa, how could you keep something like this from me?"

"I'm so sorry" was all she could say. My breaths grew short like I was going to hyperventilate. I suddenly felt an urgent need to throw something. But I just covered my mouth in awe. My stomach felt nauseous as mental pictures of Damian and Janel having sex invaded my brain. I was too stunned to cry. I stared at a piece of the carpet on the floor in a daze as the images in my head got more and more vivid.

"Oh, my God," I finally said.

Vanessa scooted toward my side of the couch and reached out to hug me. I jumped off the couch and moved away from her like she was kryptonite. "I think you need to go home," I said in voice much calmer than I should've been able to muster. "I can't believe you would wait so long to tell me this."

"Destiny, please don't be upset with me for telling you."

"I'm upset at you for *not* telling me, Vanessa! Do you know how much time I've spent crying over…"

Tears choked me and the lump in my throat threatened to erupt from my neck.

"I've been crying and praying and worrying about this man for months, and you've known all this time that he was sleeping with Janel behind my back! I can't even explain how hurt I am…by all of you!"

I ran up to my sister's bedroom as stinging tears escaped from my eyes. I heard Vanessa cry out for me to wait, but my best friend had suddenly become my enemy. I wanted nothing to do with her.

"Angel!" I yelled as I banged on her bedroom door. I heard music playing on the other side of the door. "I want you to get her out of here!" Angel unlocked her bedroom door and looked astonished at my presence.

"What's wrong?" she asked.

I pushed past her, shut the door behind me and locked it. I rushed over to Angel's bed as if I was a child running from a monster.

Angel hurried to my side after turning down her stereo.

"What's the matter, Shutter?"

My sobs were too uncontrollable for me to speak. Angel stroked my face and held me tight until I was audible.

"Vanessa, j-just told me that…Damian…he cheated on me. With Janel."

"With Janel! Your friend, Janel?"

I nodded. "Make her leave, Angel."

"Vanessa? Why do you want her leave?"

"Because she's known about this for months and she's just now telling me!" I wailed. "Damian's been calling me all this time, telling me he loved me, and I was about to take him back! How could she keep this from me?"

I buried my face in Angel's pillow and cried as Angel rubbed my back in silence. A few moments passed then I felt Angel get up. She sighed deeply then closed the door behind her as she left the room.

I was alone with my tears and my horrible imagination. I was sick at the thought of Damian kissing another woman, let alone Janel. The thought of him touching her the way he used to touch me jolted my nerves. My sobs occasionally turned to dry heaves.

How could I not have known? Did Damian ever love me, or had he always wanted Janel? How could Janel do that to me after everything I've given her and done for her? How could Vanessa not tell me? How could she say she's my friend and let me walk around so blindly? Not only had I lost the man I thought I wanted a future with, I had lost my two best friends who had lied to me and kept the most horrifying secret I ever could've imagined. This is not the way things were supposed to turn out!

Is this what I get for not going to church today, Lord?

CHAPTER 10

Heavy

Hours later, I woke up in Angel's bed feeling like my head had been smashed against a dashboard. It took awhile for me to gain enough emotional strength to leave her room and venture back downstairs. And when I did, I saw Angel sitting on the couch in the dark watching T.V. Vanessa was nowhere in sight.

I slowly shuffled over to the couch and sat down next to Angel, slightly startling her.

"Oh! I didn't hear you get up. Come here," she said, wrapping her arm around me.

I laid my head on her lap while she soothingly rubbed my back, and I felt comforted.

"Are you hungry, Shutterbug? I made your favorite."

"I'll eat in a little while," I said weakly.

We spent the next few minutes watching the dramatic ending to an HBO movie before speaking again.

"When did she leave?" I asked.

"Around six. She was hoping you would come down to talk to her."

"Whatever."

"Hop up. I'm gonna fix you a plate. You haven't eaten dinner yet."

I reluctantly sat up and let Angel go to the kitchen. My eyes felt dry and puffy, and I could barely see out of them.

I heard the microwave heating up my meal, and moments later Angel brought a hot plate of chicken, macaroni and peas to me, along with a glass of her famous ice tea. I ate vigorously at first, but it didn't take long for my stomach to get full. Angel sat next to me in silence, and I felt better just having her next to me.

I placed my almost-empty plate on the backside of a magazine sitting on the coffee table. Then Angel took my hand and clasped her fingers between mine.

"Are you going to be okay going to work tomorrow?"

"I don't know," I said. I took a long pause. "I don't think I'll ever, ever get over this." Tears stung my already weathered eyes.

"Shhh. Don't say that, Sweetie. I know it hurts but you'll get past this. I promise."

***

The next week was pretty rough. It was all I could do to keep myself from breaking out in tears when my mind wasn't occupied with work; so I tried to work as much as possible, even taking on extra assignments. During my down time, I took turns despising and analyzing my relationships with Vanessa, Janel and Damian, one by one.

I wasn't as devastated by Damian's betrayal as I was with that of Janel. I guess it's typical for females to blame the other woman when their man has been unfaithful, but this went far beyond a petty catfight over a man. This was about friendship – a friendship I had cherished through four years of college. It was a constant that I always thought I would have in my life.

My friendship with Janel was based mostly on my strength and her weakness. On the surface, Janel was a stunning beauty who loved to have fun and exuded confidence. She had a knack for always getting what she wanted. But on the inside, she was a broken, frightened little girl who searched desperately for someone to love her and take care of her.

I found myself being the one she ran to when she needed shelter from the pain of her mother's selfishness or her father's abandonment. She came to me when she needed anything - advice or a prayer, someone to be by her side when no one else was there. It was a relationship of give and take, with Janel doing all the taking. But this time, she had taken too much. There was no way I'd ever be able to forgive her for being so careless about my feelings, when all I'd ever done for her was encourage her and look out for her well-being.

As for Damian, I was glad that I no longer had to wrestle with my feelings about him. I was relieved - angry, but relieved. I now had a hard and fast reason for finally ridding him from my heart. Aside from the obvious demerits he earned from sleeping with my friend, Damian was never the man I needed him to be. I had to fight hard to trust him. I had to guard my feelings and suppress the needs of my spirit. I was never really at peace with my decision to keep him in my life and mold him into something he wasn't. But, now, it was time for him to go.

He left several messages on my answering machine, but I never called him back. I didn't quite know how to tell him that his little secret was out, and he had absolutely no chance of earning my forgiveness. I played out the eventual confrontation in my mind, though I couldn't decide if I should cuss him out, play it cool or land somewhere in the middle.

Vanessa called me everyday that week and left apologies on my voicemail. I cried every time I listened to a new one. In my heart, I knew that I shouldn't disown Vanessa for telling me the truth, even though I wished she had told me. I just wasn't ready to forgive her yet. I associated her with the news that destroyed what little bit of faith I had in love, and it weakened my confidence in our friendship.

***

I slept in late the next Saturday. An early morning thunderstorm swayed my decision to stay in bed longer than I needed to. If the fullness of my bladder hadn't propelled me out of bed, I probably never would've left the comfort of my snug haven.

After I'd relieved myself, I headed to the living room, sat myself on the couch, and turned on the television. My bare legs were cold, so I covered them with a chenille blanket we kept under the couch.

Angel was banging around pots and pans in the kitchen, wearing a pink satin robe with a silk wrap around her hair. Soon an aroma of sausage and eggs filled the room. I sat mesmerized by the television until I heard Angel say that breakfast, or as late as it was, lunch was ready.

I carried myself to the kitchen with the blanket still wrapped around me. Angel already had two places set at the table, complete with orange juice, sausage, eggs and Grand biscuits. I bowed my head as Angel asked God to bless our meal, then we began to eat.

"How are you feeling today?" asked Angel, as she tore off a piece of her biscuit.

I searched for a word to describe my mood accurately.

"Heavy," I answered.

"Ah, I remember that feeling."

"What do you mean?"

"You remember Carter, don't you? He made me feel heavy a time or two," she said.

"Oh, yeah. You two dated for almost two years, right? I don't think I ever knew why you broke up."

"I didn't talk much about it because I was too embarrassed."

"What happened?" I asked with genuine interest.

"Hummm. Well, Carter and I didn't just date. We were talking about getting married. That is, until I found out that he was already married to someone else and had a three-year-old daughter."

I gasped.

"What? Oh, my God. He kept that from you for two years?"

"No. Just one. He should've won some kind of award for keeping a secret that huge. But he had his own apartment and everything. I never suspected that he had another life apart from me. Maybe I didn't want to see it. When I finally found out, I should've left him. But he kept feeding me promises that he was getting a divorce. I tortured myself, going back and forth about my relationship with him, when deep down, I knew that things would never be right between us. I thought Carter was so perfect. I thought I would never find love like that again, so I was afraid to let him go."

"What made you finally leave him?" I asked, completely engulfed in her story.

"I fought it for a long time, but I eventually got tired of being the other woman. I knew I deserved better. And if I held on to something that wasn't mine, I would miss what God had for me. So, I left him."

"Wow. I don't know how you keep such a positive outlook on love after going through something like that. I mean, that was years ago."

"Well, Shutterbug, just because you have a nightmare doesn't mean you should stop dreaming."

"That sounds like something Mama would say," I said, suddenly wishing I could go home and cry in my mother's arms. But Angel was a pretty good substitute.

"It's true. It's the greatest thing about having faith. No matter how much pain you're in, or how dark your days might be, you always have hope that things will get better. And they did. I eventually moved on."

"Don't you ever get lonely?"

"Sure I do. But I will never let loneliness drive me into the arms of the wrong man. I believe that what God has for me belongs to me and no one else. I just have to be patient because it will be worth it."

"I want what God has for me," I said, earnestly.

"He will give it to you - in His own perfect timing. And I promise you when it comes, you will know. There will be no doubt in your mind when you've found the right one."

"I love you, Angel. You're the only friend I have left," I said.

"That's not true, and you know it. That's all I'm going to say about that," she said, with loving attitude.

"Yeah, I know. I'm going to call Vanessa soon. I just need this wound to close up a little."

***

I spent most of the day balled up on the couch under a blanket, watching movies on Lifetime and HBO. It was pitiful, but I had no energy to go anywhere or do anything. Angel, on the other hand, had a date with some guy named Walter that she met in a bookstore. She told me she felt guilty leaving me at home feeling depressed while she was out being sociable, but I insisted that she should go and have a good time.

"Are you sure you don't want me to stay home? I can pick up some movies and order a pizza," she said thoughtfully.

"No, it's okay. I'll be fine." My tone was flat, but convincing. There was no way I would've kept Angel from having a good time that night. At least *one* of us deserved to be happy.

Angel looked so pretty. Her hair was straight and silky, and she wore black capris with a black and white top. She smelled heavenly, as usual. She almost inspired me to want to go out...almost.

Around seven-thirty that night, I decided to take a long, hot shower and wash my hair in water that stayed just bearable enough not to scald me. Steam filled the bathroom, and I tried to escape into a mini paradise. I began to lather my hair, but stopped suddenly when I swore I heard the doorbell ringing. I pulled back the shower curtain and listened again. Nothing.

I finished rinsing the shampoo, conditioner and soap off my hair and body, toweled down and put on my robe. There was the doorbell again.

"Who in the world?" I asked aloud as I scurried to the door. I looked out of the peephole. Someone's finger was covering it up.

"Who is it?" I asked, annoyed.

"It's Damian, Baby. Let me in. I've been standing out here for ten minutes."

I never imagined my eventual confrontation with Damian would take place this soon, in person, and with me in my robe with wet hair. Without thinking, I flung the door open and saw Damian holding a dozen roses with a smile on his face. I went numb.

Damian hugged me up in his arms, twirled me around then put me down. My robe almost came undone.

"These are for you," he said, handing me the roses. "You look great, by the way. The wet thing works for you."

"What are you doing here?" I asked, still shocked at my unexpected interruption.

"I told you I was coming to see you, Baby. I guess you got too busy to return any of my phone calls so I decided just to surprise you."

"I *am* surprised," I said astonished. I smelled the roses out of instinct.

"I missed you so much, Baby. Come here."

He took my face in his hands and dropped a moist kiss on my mouth before I knew what was happening. I pushed him away, though, and tried to remind myself that was the man I was supposed to hate.

"The place looks nice," Damian continued as if nothing was wrong. He came further into the condo and inspected the place like he was considering a purchase.

"Damian, sit down. We need to talk," I said sternly. I closed the door and headed to the couch before my knees could give out on me.

"What do you want to talk about?"

"Just come and sit down," I said with a sigh. I really wasn't ready for this conversation yet.

"Okay, I'm sitting," he said after finding a seat among the pile of blankets and pillows I had left on the couch. "But I have to admit. I was expecting a little more affection after driving five hours to see the woman I love."

I sat across from him, roses in hand, and I looked into his face – his wonderfully handsome face – and for a second I wanted to kiss him again. I wanted this whole thing to be a big joke. Ha, ha. I wanted more than anything for things to be right between us. But like Angel said, if I tried to hold on to something that wasn't mine, I'd be blocking my own blessings.

"I know about you and Janel." Her name sounded shrill in my ears when I said it.

Awkward silence filled the space between us. I waited for him to deny it, or explain it. But he just sat there, biting his thumbnails. So I figured it would be a good time to get some things off my chest.

"You can't even imagine how much you've devastated me, Damian. I was trying so hard to make things work with you. But you continue to break my heart. So if that was your goal, congratulations. Now you can take these meaningless roses, get back in your car, drive back to North Carolina and sleep with my ex-friend, Janel, with a free conscience. I don't ever want to see you again. I don't want you to call me. Just forget you ever knew me."

I stood to my feet and went to open the door. But when I looked back, he was still sitting motionless on the couch.

"I'd like you to leave now," I said, sounding much stronger than I felt.

"Can I just say something?" he asked, as if I owed him that right.

"No! I want you to go!" My voice began to quiver, but I didn't want to give him the satisfaction of seeing me cry.

"Please, Destiny. Come sit down." His tone softened. "I just want to talk to you."

I thought about causing a scene and making him leave, but I really did want to hear what he had to say. I needed my two-year love affair to end with some sort of peace of mind. So I tossed the roses onto the coffee table and made my way back to the couch across from him again.

"Make it quick. I have some place to be," I lied.

Damian sighed and bit his bottom lip before speaking.

"Vanessa told you, didn't she?"

His comment stung. It just confirmed that the whole thing wasn't a joke.

"It doesn't matter how I found out. I'm just glad I know the truth about you," I sneered.

"The truth is I love you, and I want to be with you more than anything. I've made some mistakes in the past but I'm not the same person anymore."

"Oh, really? When did you make this big change? Because from what I heard you were with her the day I left, which would be, oh, two months ago."

"It just happened, Baby" I never cared about her," he said with confidence, as if it made his actions excusable.

"Well that makes you a real winner, Damian! You slept with Janel without caring about her. What does that say about you, huh? What does that say about me? Did you ever care about me?"

"You know I love you, Baby. Don't ever think that I didn't."

"Stop saying that! You don't love me at all. Whatever happened to *'you're the only woman I want'*?"

"You are the only…"

"Oh, please, Damian! If you loved me so much then why wasn't I enough?" I asked, almost screaming. "Was she just prettier than me? Have you always secretly wanted Janel? Or was it just because she would give it up when I wouldn't?"

"Don't say that."

"Why not?! It's true, isn't it? You had every right to sleep with someone else because I was holding out on you! Is that right?!" I yelled.

Then there was a painful silence. I couldn't control my tears any longer. They gushed down my face.

"Why was I not enough for you?" I asked through tears. "If you truly loved me, and I was truly the only woman for you, you would have waited for me. No one else could have taken my place."

"I'm sorry, Baby," Damian said, defeated.

"And with my *best friend*, Damian? My *best friend*. How could you betray me like that? I can't believe that someone I loved so much could do that to me."

"Destiny, you are everything to me…"

"No, Damian, stop. I accept the simple fact that I wasn't enough for you. And you have never been enough for me. I'm not wasting another minute on you."

I wanted so badly to confront him without emotion, but I should've known better. I had given him my everything, and it hurt so badly that he was willing to give it to someone else.

"I wish I could take it all back, Baby. I'm sorry."

Damian's deep, charming voice was replaced with a quivering vibrato trying to hide evidence of tears. "Is there any way I can make you forgive me? I'll do whatever you ask me. Baby, I need you in my life."

"What you need is to get your life together. And what I need is for you to leave."

I stood up and glared at him until he followed me to the door. But when I opened it, he grabbed me and hugged me tight, letting out loud cries.

"I'm sorry, Baby. I never meant to hurt you. I love you so much," he sobbed.

I lost all strength in my legs and practically went limp in his arms. His embrace soothed me and disgusted me all at the same time, and my heart was shattering all over the floor.

"Just let me go," I begged, overwhelmed with tears. "I need you to stay away from me. Just get away from me."

Wrapped in a whirlwind of love and unspeakable pain, we stood at the door, embracing for what seemed like an eternity. And when Damian finally left, I was sad, but I no longer felt heavy.

CHAPTER 11

Hemorrhoids

"Destiny, which one of these do you think would work better for that 'Generous Juror' story?"

"Huh?" I asked, snapping out of my daze. I was supposed to be downloading photos from my camera onto the share drive in the office, but ended up staring at the screen like I was hypnotized. I glanced over at Aileen who held out a page of prints with two photos circled.

"What's the story?" I asked, taking the proof sheet from her and examining the photos.

"Are you doing all right? You haven't really been yourself lately," Aileen noticed. A sincere look of concern was etched on her colorless forty-something face as she peered at me over her glasses.

"Oh, I'm fine. Thanks for asking," I said shortly. I didn't take my eyes off the proof sheet. I never made it a point to discuss my personal life with people at work and I wasn't going to break that habit today.

"Are you sure?"

"Yeah, I'm fine. Just fine."

"Well, Destiny, you think about this the next time you get to feeling down." Aileen leaned over me, her mousy-brown hair and gold necklace drooping into my space. "All you have to do when you're having a hard time is to think of all the other people in the world who have it much worse than you. Take me, for example," she said, placing her hand on her chest. "My husband told me he wants a divorce. I just found out my kid is on drugs. And I have the worst case of hemorrhoids you could possibly fathom."

My eyes widened in astonishment. Was this lady serious? I didn't know whether to laugh at her cruel joke or run away from her.

Aileen gave me a devilish little wink.

"Just kidding," she smiled. "But I hope it made you feel better."

Aileen pushed her glasses back to their proper position on her face and turned to walk away. She was a strange old bird, but she did make me feel better, even if it was just for a second.

I had spent the last few weeks crying so much that I had no moisture left in my body. I tried not to let my sadness show at work, or even too much around Angel. The spirit of depression banged on my door every night, but I refused to let it in. I couldn't help but feel knocked down by my turn of events, though. I felt like I might never get over what Damian and Janel did to me.

I was starting to get tired of my pity party. I worked all the time, never socialized, and in the past month I had gained at least five pounds and an inch of fleshy flab around my waist. I decided it was time for a change. After all, it wasn't the end of the world. At least my kid wasn't on drugs and I didn't have hemorrhoids, right?

I grabbed my healing process by the horns and decided that the first step to my recovery would be to reconcile my relationship with Vanessa. I wasn't sure how she would respond to an apology for not returning any of her numerous phone calls, but I swallowed my pride, and called her anyway.

Vanessa still shared an apartment with Janel, so I only had a fifty-fifty chance of getting her on the phone. I dialed their number and prayed Janel wouldn't pick up. I wasn't ready to deal with her just yet.

"Hello?" Vanessa answered.

"Hey, lady," I said in my customary fashion.

"Destiny? Oh, my God! I'm so glad you called. How have you been?"

"I'm hanging in there." I felt the tears coming already. "Look, Nessa, I really just wanted to apologize for not returning your calls. It's taken me awhile to process everything that happened..."

"Don't even worry about it," she interrupted sternly. "You don't have to explain anything."

"Yes, I do," I insisted, although I was thankful she wasn't upset with me. "I shouldn't have treated you the way I did after you drove all the way to Baltimore to see me. I should've thanked you for telling me. I may never have found out if you hadn't said anything."

"Don't sweat it, Girl. I'm just glad we're talking again."

"Me, too. I've missed you." A wave of relief rode through me as I realized I had my friend back.

"Are you doing okay?" she asked.

"Yeah, I'm okay. Tell me what's been going on with you."

"Well, I'm glad you called today because I'm moving into my new apartment in Raleigh this weekend. I already have my new number if you want it."

"Of course, but why are you moving out? I hope it's not because of your loyalty to me. I understand if you still need her as a roommate to save money."

"The move is not just because of what Janel did to you, even though it played a big part. But you know we had problems with our living arrangement way before all this. Besides, Rodney and I picked out the new place together and he's moving in with me just as soon as we get married. It's all for the best."

"I'm glad to hear things are working out for you, Nessa."

"And I'm glad to hear your voice. I've been worried about you."

When I got off the phone with Vanessa, everything seemed right with the world again. Well, almost everything. Now it was time to move on to step two.

Five days a week for at least thirty minutes a day, I was as committed to my workout routine as George W. Bush was committed to invading Iraq. I joined a fitness center only five minutes away from the condo. And as hard as it was to drag myself to the gym after a long day at work, the results were worth it.

I forced myself to do sets of sit-ups every night before bed, drink plenty of water, and cut back on all the fast food I had been eating. It only took two weeks to firm up my waist, and I was actually starting to see some of the muscle tone I had back when I was a young athlete in high school. Angel was so impressed she started going to the gym with me.

One particular evening, Angel and I were changing clothes so we could go to the gym when I heard the phone ring. I picked up the phone and a glanced at the caller ID number which was the same as the number for Vanessa and Janel's apartment.

"Hey, Girl!" I answered, completely expecting to hear Vanessa on the other end.

"Destiny?" asked the voice timidly. My nerves clinched as I sorted through my memory bank and recognized Janel's voice.

"Yes, this is Destiny," I said, wanting to make her identify herself.

"Hey, Girl. It's Janel. How have you been?" she asked, testing the waters.

As quick as the flip of a light switch, my blood began to boil and my tongue was ready to aim and fire. "I was doing a lot better before I found out my best friend was having sex with my boyfriend," I stabbed. All the tears and pain I had suffered in the past months had hardened into anger, and I was surprisingly thankful for the opportunity to direct that anger at the person who deserved it most.

"I know you probably hate me," Janel began. "But I just wanted to tell you that I'm sorry."

"I know you're sorry, Janel! You're a sorry excuse for a woman and a sorry excuse for a friend!" I expected Janel to hang up at any minute, but she stayed on the phone and took my verbal abuse.

"I hope it was good to you, Janel. I hope sleeping with Damian was worth losing your friend over because I will never forgive you for what you put me through. To me, you don't even exist anymore. I'm just sad that I wasted so many years calling you my friend. Clearly you don't know the meaning of the word. So let me educate you on the definition. A friend is what I used to be to you. And a friend is someone who would never, ever do what you did to me. So now that we are no longer friends, I really don't have anything else to say to you. Don't you *ever* call me again!"

"I'm so sorry, Destiny!" Janel cried.

"Save the tears for someone who cares. I don't anymore. Why don't you go cry on Damian's shoulder."

I hung up the phone, feeling a strange sense of pride for telling Janel off. She was so manipulative! Did she really think a phone call and a weak 'I'm sorry' would erase all the heartache she caused? And if she was really sorry, why did it take her so long to call? The only reason she called is because she probably needed me to do something for her, the selfish…oooh, she made me so sick!

I spent the rest of the night replaying the conversation over and over in my head, wishing I had said more. Now that I knew she cared enough to call, I felt like I might be able to move forward with my life.

Speaking of moving forward, Mrs. Watson's son, Jonathon called me the next night and asked me out on a date for that Friday at a restaurant called Jasper's. I gladly accepted, considering the date as a sign that things were beginning to look up. Vanessa was back in my life, I was getting in shape and finding new ways to spend my time in Baltimore. I felt like I was making moves in the right direction. Still, there were nights when I'd lie in bed crying and praying for God to remove the unyielding pain that lingered in my heart caused by two people who had meant so much to me. All I had was the hope that things were getting better.

Serena K. Wallace

CHAPTER 12

Julius "J.T." Walker

My life was full, but it was still missing something. It was missing that extra something that makes you race out of bed every morning, anxious to start your day. But the first time I saw Destiny's face, I realized that I was ready for that extra something.

It was a cold night early in November when Destiny showed up at a high school basketball game I was coaching, but that wasn't the first time I had seen her. It all started last Friday when I was rounding up my week tutoring a student of mine who was struggling in pre-calculus.

"I'm just not getting it, Mr. Walker. How am I supposed to get into college if I can't pass your stupid class?" asked Amber, a pale-faced brunette in her senior year of high school.

"Stupid class, huh? My class is not stupid and neither are my students," I said. "Now, you can do this work, Amber. I've seen you do it. Let's walk through this one more time."

I spent the next twenty minutes helping Amber re-work two of the problems she missed on her calculus exam. The look of confusion and frustration slowly began to melt from her face as she talked herself through the problem.

"See," I said. "You *can* handle this class. I know that you're trying hard, so come back here Monday after school and I'll have some extra credit problems for you to work on."

"Thanks, Teach. I'll see you Monday."

When Amber left my classroom, I hastily crammed my grade book and homework folders into my brief case and straightened the clutter on my desk. I hated starting a new week with a messy work space, so I always took a few minutes each Friday to make it look halfway organized. Just as I'd finished packing my belongings, Mrs. Hanson's tall, slender silhouette appeared in the doorway. She was a blonde, blue-eyed English teacher in her thirties who had been shamelessly flirting with me ever since I started teaching at Mercer.

"Julius, I'm glad I caught you before practice," she said in a sultry voice. I hated being called Julius, and I didn't have time for her games today. I was already late.

"What can I do for you, Mrs. Hanson?"

"I told you to call me Karen when there are no students around." She winked at me then sashayed over to my desk. "I just wanted to bring you these," she said, handing me several orange flyers advertising a county-wide college fair.

"Thank you. I'll be sure to post these. Now, if you will excuse me. I'm running a little late."

"Anything for you, Julius."

"Please, call me Mr. Walker – even when there are no students around."

I hurried Karen, I mean, Mrs. Hanson out of my classroom, turned out the light and shut the door behind me, briefcase and gym bag in hand. The hallways, now deserted, were usually swarming with zit-faced teenagers with raging hormones. It wasn't uncommon to find myself having to separate a few young couples engaged in lip locks in the hallways after school. But I loved my job and wouldn't be anywhere else but here.

Two years ago, I was a senior at the University of Maryland with dreams of becoming an NBA player. But being a benchwarmer for the Terps didn't get me much attention from scouts. So, I graduated and pursued Plan B: teaching pre-calculus and trigonometry and assisting the varsity basketball coach at Mercer High School. At times, I felt like I bit off more than I could chew between staff meetings, tutoring sessions and ball practice, but I was doing what made me happy, and the challenge kept me going.

I glanced at my watch as I shuffled down the steps and rounded the corner to the gym. I figured Coach Maze probably had the boys good and warm by now.

"Coach! You're late!" Jamal yelled teasingly, bouncing a basketball down the court.

"You just keep running, Young Buck! Don't worry about me!"

Jamal was the star player of the basketball team, a good kid whose looks and skills on the court made him a little cocky. I knew from personal experience that basketball was not enough to get by, so I took it upon myself to make sure he didn't get too full of himself and that he kept his grades up.

I tried to look after all my kids - my players and my students. There's nothing worse than a student with all the potential in the world falling through the cracks because no one invested any time in him. I figured if I could keep one kid on the right path, every headache that came with teaching was worth it.

After two hours of running my boys on the court and going over the schedule with Coach Maze, I packed up my bags and headed home on the Baltimore/Washington Parkway. I was exhausted after a long week of math and basketball - two of my favorite things in the world. But now, all I wanted to do was relax. I was supposed to go out with some of my friends that night, but I was tired and didn't feel like doing anything but crashing on the couch and watching movies until I passed out. It looked like it was going to be yet another Blockbuster night.

When I got home, I dumped my briefcase and gym bag on the floor and went into the kitchen for something to drink. I pulled a bottle of Gatorade out of the fridge and swallowed everything that was left before tossing the bottle in the trash. Red was my favorite.

The message light on my phone was flashing, so I picked it up and checked my voicemail. One message was from my little brother, Xavier, who was a sophomore at Princeton University. The other message was from my ex-girlfriend.

"J.T., this is Shayla," she said in her creamy smooth voice. "I just wanted to see how you've been doing. I miss you. You haven't called me in awhile, so hit me back when you get a chance, okay. Take care."

Odds were that I wasn't going to call her back. It had been about four months since I'd broken up with Shayla- one of the hardest things I've ever had to do. She was a beautiful woman and we had a lot of fun during the year that we dated. Things took a nasty turn, however, when our conversations turned to marriage. As much as I loved having Shayla as a girlfriend, I knew she wasn't meant to be my wife. I just wish I hadn't been so honest with her by telling her that fact. No woman wants to hear that she's not "the one." I should've just lied and told her that I was seeing someone else. But the truth was that I hadn't found everything I wanted and needed in a wife in her. And it wasn't fair for me to continue to waste her time or mine.

Shayla took the break-up pretty hard, and I had to admit I missed her sometimes. But it was all for the best. We had both started dating other people, but she still called me from time to time. Ever since the break-up, my friend Tony was always trying to get me to go to clubs with him and pick up women, which was cool the first eight thousand times we did it. But the club scene had lost its novelty back in my junior year of college. So now, most of my free time was spent working out or watching T.V. at home.

I mentally disregarded Shayla's call, and dialed my brother's dorm room.

"Hello?" he answered.

"What's up, Genius?"

"What's up?"

"You never call me unless you need something, so what do you want? Talk to me," I joked.

"I can't just call my big brother to say 'hello'?"

"No. Now spit it out."

"Okay. Okay. I need some money," Xavier admitted.

"Money for what?"

"I have a date tomorrow night and need some money to take this girl out."

"A date?" I asked, thoroughly elated. "Since when do you have time for girls?"

"I don't. But there's this one girl I kinda like. And she told me she likes me. So I asked her for a date."

"My baby brother, The Mack! It's about time you took your nose out of the books for a second and enjoyed yourself. Tell me about this girl."

I was so proud of my brother I could burst. He had always been an academic wizard, but when it came to girls, he came into the game late. Very late. I didn't want him to be one of those socially inept geniuses. To me, life was all about healthy balance.

I listened to my brother tell me about this girl he liked and promised him I would wire him some money. When we got off the phone, I went into my bedroom, fell onto my bed and dozed off within minutes. I drifted into one of those deep, wonderful power naps that refresh you like you've slept for days, but I was interrupted by the sound of the phone ringing at about eight o'clock.

"Hello?"

"J.T. What's up, Man? You going out with us tonight?" asked my friend, Tony.

"To Jasper's?"

"Yeah."

"Naw, Man. I think I'll pass. It's been a long week."

"Come on, Man. Andre got a promotion and he wants us to help him celebrate."

"For real?" I yawned. "All right, that's cool. I'll be there."

"All right, Man."

"All right."

I hung up the phone just as my stomach began to grumble. I couldn't wait to get something to eat. After a hot shower, I shaved away my five o'clock shadow and put on some slacks and a blue dress shirt. I gave myself a once-over before putting on my jacket and heading to the restaurant.

Jasper's was an after-work hang out spot where a lot of urban professionals went to unwind. I walked inside, observing the happy crowd of friends and lovers eating, drinking and celebrating the end of their busy weeks. The place was pretty full, but it wasn't hard to spot my big-headed friends perched on stools at the bar, bantering back and forth about this and that.

"Aaaay, J.T.! Get over here, Man!" yelled Tony. "I'm glad you decided to join the Land of the Living."

"You're just glad I'm here 'cause you think I'm gonna drive you drunk fools home."

"You got that right, Son," Tony bellowed. They all laughed.

"Congrats on the promotion, Man," I said to Andre.

"Thanks, Man. But I've got some even better news," he said.

I took a seat next to Andre who immediately brought me up to speed on his story about this woman he'd been pining over for months who finally gave him the time of day.

Andre was a financial advisor with a major investment company in D.C. If it wasn't for him, I might not have graduated from college. He was my wing man in the math department at the University of Maryland and helped me make it through some tough courses. He was ridiculously smart, but he needed a few more lessons when it came to women. That's where Tony and I came in.

I had known Tony, the loud one, ever since I was in high school, and we were frat brothers in college. He always messed with me about getting all the girls, but he was the real ladies' man. Although he might not always be the prettiest brother in the room, women were attracted to his sense of humor and the way he carried himself. It also helped that he was a sports agent who rubbed elbows with all types of celebrities.

If I had to pick the quiet one of the group, it would have to be Chris. He didn't talk a lot, but when he did, he always said something profound. Chris was an architect by day, musician by night, playing bass guitar for a local jazz band. Chris was a renaissance brother who loved all kinds of art and music. Dude was always dragging us to plays and museums. And he was the only one of us who was married.

I laughed and carried on with the guys while I sipped on a Coke and waited for the plate of hot wings and fries I had ordered. As I faded in and out of the conversation, my eyes searched the room for something interesting to look at. I was a people-watcher. I liked hypothesizing stories and observing how people interact with one another. You can tell a lot about people if you just pay attention.

I noticed a light-skinned black man and an attractive Asian woman dining together, engrossed in their conversation. My guess was that they had been dating for a few weeks and the newness of the relationship had not yet worn off. At the far end of the establishment, three sisters were cackling and joking with one another. I caught them eyeing the four of us sitting at the bar.

The awkward interaction of the Caucasian foursome sitting at the table to my left helped me deduce that they were on a double-date. Then I glanced over at an older, brown-haired man sitting alone reading a novel. I guessed that he was an amateur writer who fed himself a steady diet of reading material to stay current in his field.

A moment later, my analysis was distracted by a brown-skinned beauty in a black dress, making her way to the only empty booth in the room.

"Do you see that?" said Andre, in mid-sentence of his long story. I could tell I wasn't the only one whose radar had found a target.

The beauty settled into the booth then ran her eyes around the room as if she were looking for someone. I silently wished she was looking for me. I'm not usually one to get crazy over a beautiful woman. I'd seen plenty in my day. But for some reason I couldn't help but watch her as she ordered a drink and perused the menu. It was hard to make out much detail in her face, but from a distance she was breathtaking. Her eyes were dark and her skin glowed under the dim lamp above her table. Her hair, black and shiny, rested softly on her bare shoulders.

I tried to snap myself out of my fixation and struck up a new conversation with Tony, Chris, and Andre while I feasted on the wings and fries the waitress finally placed in front of me. I caught myself sneaking peeks at the mysterious angel throughout my meal, though. Our eyes met briefly before she turned away, obviously nervous at the sight of the four of us staring at her like she was the first woman we'd ever seen.

This woman didn't look like she was from around here. It's not like I knew every female in the city, but there was a doe-like innocence in her face like she was new not only to the restaurant, but to the people and the vibe of her surroundings. I wondered what her story was.

Out of the blue, Andre, with his newfound confidence, rose from his bar stool and starting walking toward the lone princess.

"What does this fool think he's doing?" asked Tony.

We all watched in silence as the scene played out. Andre, with his short, stocky self, stood next to her table and spoke to the lady in black for a few moments. She smiled a gorgeous white smile at him then politely shook his hand. After a brief exchange, Andre held up his hand as if to say "My bad." And she smiled at him one more time before he came back to his seat.

"Ah, Man. She's waiting for some dude," said Andre, as if he was surprised that she would be expecting someone.

"What did you think she was doing?" asked Tony. "You've got to be one of the dumbest brothers I know!"

We clowned Andre about his elementary dating skills then moved on to other topics of conversation. During that time, the beauty's date arrived, and I could see him pouring out apologies to her for being late. My analysis: a first date - probably a first date that wouldn't lead to a second.

I finished my food and paid the bill before bidding my boys a good evening. I'd decided I was too tired to go to the club with them, and of course, they ragged me and called me an old man. But before I left my seat, I tossed a question to Andre to quench my curiosity.

"Hey, Andre. Did you at least get her name, man?"

"Yeah, I did."

I grabbed a toothpick out of the dispenser on the bar then told the guys to catch a cab if they were too faded to drive home. As I left the restaurant, I stole one last glance at the beauty and her nerdy-looking date before walking out the door and into the crisp autumn wind. I got in my car and headed back to my apartment. I couldn't wait to get home, go to sleep, and dream of the woman in the black dress named Destiny.

CHAPTER 13

Only In My Dreams

It turned out that my blind date with Jonathon Watson was a complete waste of life. Talk about holding your breath for nothing! Not only was he thirty minutes late, but an hour into our meal he admitted that he was in love with another woman who lived in Atlanta! Apparently, his mother didn't like this girl. So, he only agreed to go on a date with me to get his mommy off his back. What a baby! It was kind of funny, though. When I got home and told Angel about it, she reminded me that as long as I got a free meal, the date was a success.

My dating track record was zero for two, but the pendulum of Angel's love life was on the upswing. Walter, the guy she met at the bookstore, was officially her new beau, and they had been dating for a few months now. I liked Walter. He treated my sister like a queen and had her beaming like a glow worm all the time.

Walter's stature resembled that of a pro football player who carried himself with great presence. His skin looked cocoa-butter smooth and his hair was coal black and wavy. He was a graduate of the Air Force Academy and was now stationed at Andrews Air Force Base, MD where he was awaiting pilot training.

"This is some good stuff," he said, flipping through my portfolio one Friday evening. He was waiting on the couch in the living room for Angel to get dressed for a date.

"I still have a lot to learn, but it's a good start," I said modestly.

"Do you do any freelance work?"

"Not as much as I should. I'd like to shoot weddings and stuff, but I've been working on Saturdays lately. I eventually want to start my own business, though."

"You're a talented young lady," Walter observed. "I know a lot of people who might want to use your services one day. You should get some business cards made."

"Yeah, Angel tells me that all the time. She's such the entrepreneur."

Just then, Angel came downstairs dressed in jeans and a red sweater with her hair pulled up in a tussled ponytail.

"I'm ready, Baby. Just let me put on my boots," she said to Walter.

"Where are you two lovebirds heading tonight?" I asked.

Walter responded, "My cousin has a game tonight and we're going to watch him play. He's a power forward on the basketball team at Mercer."

"Mercer?" I asked.

"Mercer High School. Hey, do you like basketball?"

"Yeah, I used to play a little back in the day," I reminisced.

"You should come with us tonight," Walter offered.

"Nooo. I wouldn't dare intrude on your date. I wasn't made to be a third wheel."

"Come on, Shutterbug," Angel chimed in. "It'll be fun. You don't have any plans tonight, do you?"

"Not really, but…"

Walter interrupted. "Don't consider yourself to be the third wheel, okay? Let's say you're on assignment."

"What?" I asked, puzzled.

"Well, I was trying to think of a polite way to ask, but I was hoping you might be willing to take some photos of my cousin during his game. My aunt's always complaining about how her pictures never turn out right. Maybe I could pay you to take some good ones for me."

"You wouldn't have to pay me for that. I'd love to."

"Great!" said Angel as she put on her second boot. "Now, go get dressed! We have to hurry if we're going to get good seats."

***

It felt like it had been a million years since I'd stepped foot into a high school, even though it had only been four. An impressive crowd began filing into the gymnasium from all four corners with fans wearing a combination of red and white attire, the colors of the Mercer High School Falcons. I followed Walter and Angel up the bleacher steps, cradling my camera bag that was draped over my shoulder. We sat down next to an attractive lady with two little boys parked next to her.

"Aunt Rita," Walter began. "This is my girlfriend, Angel, and her sister, Destiny. Ladies, this is my Aunt Rita." Angel and I reached across Walter and shook his aunt's hand.

"Nice to meet you two. You're both so pretty," said Aunt Rita sweetly. "These are my grandchildren, Jesse and Nathaniel."

I smiled at the cute little boys who looked to be about three or four.

"Destiny's a professional photographer, Auntie. I asked her to come so we can get some good shots of Jamal."

Aunt Rita's face lit up. "A professional? Oh! We need to get you a better seat. My Baby is the best player on the team. He's got scouts looking at him and everything. Come with me."

Before I could blink, Aunt Rita stood up and beckoned me to follow her. I glanced at Angel, then Walter, who gave me the "okay" with his eyes. I trailed a few steps behind Aunt Rita down the bleachers as she led me to the side of the court.

"Coach Walker!" she called out to a tall man in a gray suit with his back to us. The man turned around and my heart nearly skipped a beat. He was beautiful.

"Miss Dunbar, how are you doing?" he asked, smiling a ridiculously gorgeous smile.

"I'm wonderful," said Aunt Rita. "Walter brought a professional photographer to take pictures of Jamal for me. What's your name again, Sweetheart," she asked, shifting her gaze toward me.

"Destiny." I flashed a bright smile and stretched my hand toward the handsome stranger.

"Julius Walker, but please call me J.T." As he shook my hand, he squinted his eyes as if he caught a hint of familiarity in my face. "A photographer, huh?"

"Yep. I work for the *Baltimore Sun*." I silently wished I hadn't said 'yep' like a hillbilly.

Aunt Rita took me by the hand. "Would it be all right if she walked around to get some good shots? Or maybe we could get her a seat near the court."

"I don't see why not. You can sit or stand wherever you like, Miss Destiny."

"Perfect!" said Aunt Rita. "Oh, this is wonderful!"

"Coach Walker!" yelled someone from the entryway of the locker room.

"Please excuse me, ladies," said Mr. Handsome. And just like that, he was gone.

Aunt Rita proudly informed me that her son's jersey number was 33 so I could identify him on the court. I spent the next two hours snapping away with my camera, pretending to be consumed with every dribble and every basket Jamal made. He was actually a great ball-player, but my real source of entertainment that night was watching J.T. and his fine self.

He was coaching on the sidelines next to a short, round, white guy with a brown mustache, who kept hollering commands at the team. He and J.T. balanced each other like day and night, with the round coach wearing excitement and frustration on his beet-red face, while J.T. remained cool and collected, showing little emotion.

I snuck peeks of J.T. throughout the night, captivated by his quiet power and masculinity. He had to be in his mid-twenties, at least 6 foot 3, 220 pounds, and his athletic frame was coated with luscious mahogany skin. He wore his hair cut close, and a fine mustache rested above his enticing, round lips. There was something undeniably intriguing about him, and I felt like I would burst in anticipation of talking to him again.

Near the end of the game, the crowd cheered and stomped on the wooden bleachers. It was obvious that the Falcons had already won the game with an 11-point lead and four seconds to go. Jamal, of course, was the team superstar. At the sound of the buzzer, a flood of students and fans from the home team rushed the court and celebrated with the players. I clapped and cheered, not being able to ignore the school spirit that swirled thick in the air.

After the team disappeared into the locker room and the crowd began to die down, I married up with Angel, Walter, Aunt Rita and her grandsons who were waiting for Jamal near the locker room entrance.

"That was quite a game," I said to Aunt Rita, who was beaming with pride.

"Did you get some good pictures?"

"I sure did," I responded. "He gave a great show."

The lot of us chatted for awhile about highlights of the game and how the cheerleaders looked like grown women. A few high school girls wearing letterman jackets were waiting for some of the players, which sparked comments from Aunt Rita about how many different girls had been calling her house for Jamal. Just then, J.T. and the round coach emerged from the locker room wearing windbreaker sweat suits with their names embroidered on the front.

"There she is! The mother of my star player!" exclaimed the round coach. He hugged Aunt Rita and engaged her in a private conversation.

My eyes inevitably locked with J.T.'s, and I felt like we were the only two people in the gym; that is, until Walter reminded me that we weren't.

"Good lookin' team you got there, Coach," Walter said to J.T.

"Yeah, these boys really want it this year."

"And they'll get it too if they keep this up. They haven't lost a game yet."

The two men carried on with their basketball banter as I studied J.T., trying to burn an image of him in my memory in case I would never see him again. Angel broke my concentration by clearing her throat.

"Oh, I'm sorry, Baby," Walter said to Angel. "J.T., this is my lady,

Angel. And this is her sister, Destiny."

J.T. shook Angel's hand and said, "Nice to meet you, Angel. And Destiny, I believe we've met. Did you enjoy the game?"

"Yeah, it was great. Jamal is something else."

"Were you able to get some good shots of him?"

"Sure did," I said with confidence.

"Man, if he knew a professional photographer was here for him, we wouldn't be able to shut him up for days," he said, smiling. "I can't let him get too full of himself, you know?"

I nodded and smiled back at him.

"You have a beautiful smile," J.T. said to me, throwing me completely off guard. I blushed at his compliment as if I was thirteen. Our eyes locked again as I thanked him and flashed another smile.

"Well," said Angel, dramatically. "Walter and I will meet you at the car, Destiny. It was nice meeting you, J.T."

Angel grabbed Walter by the hand and they headed toward the exit.

"Catch you later, J.T." said Walter.

"All right, Man."

I took in a deep breath as I realized that this was the moment I had been hoping for during the past two hours – a moment alone with J.T.

"I sense that those two wanted us to be alone," he said.

"Yeah, my sister is always trying to play matchmaker."

I winced, thinking about the implications of my last statement. I didn't want J.T. to think I was desperate for a man and I needed my sister to hook me up.

J.T. bit his bottom lip and smiled during an intense moment of silence.

"What?" I asked, shyly.

"I thought I was never going to see you again."

I screwed up my face in confusion, wondering if the man I was drooling over was a complete psycho.

"Have…we met before?" I asked.

He chuckled. "Only in my dreams. Listen. I'm supposed to celebrate with the team tonight. Coach Maze and I usually take the boys for pizza after a win. But I'd like to see you again. Is there anyone in your life who would object if I called you some time?"

"No one I can think of," I said.

J.T. pulled a slim cell phone out of his pocket and keyed my home number into his phone book as I recited it to him. Then he walked me to Walter's car in the chill of the November night air as we shared a little about ourselves.

J.T. told me that he graduated from the University of Maryland with a degree in math, and he had been coaching and teaching pre-calculus and trigonometry at Mercer High School for two years. He said that he hoped to work his way up the administration chain and become a principal of a high school one day. Needless to say I was impressed with him on every level, but I still hadn't forgotten about the crazy comment he made earlier.

"What did you mean when you said you thought you would never see me again?" I asked him, just as we were approaching Walter's SUV.

He stood across from me with his hands in his coat pockets as the moon accentuated the curves of his chiseled face.

"I didn't mean to scare you when I said that," he said. "It's just that I've seen you somewhere before, and I remember thinking about you long after you were gone. I was hoping I would run into you again, and…here you are."

"You're not a stalker or anything, are you?"

"Oh! The stalker question," he said, with playful exasperation. "No, no. I wouldn't do you like that. I'll only call when you want me to call. I'll only come around when you want me around. I'm drama-free."

"Drama-free. I like that," I said, not being able to contain my smiles.

"Well, let me get you out of this cold air. I'll give you a call soon, okay?"

"Okay."

J.T. opened the door of Walter's SUV and helped me into my seat. His touch sent chills up my spine. He exchanged goodbyes with Angel and Walter then winked at me before he closed the door, sending me home with goose bumps.

Serena K. Wallace

CHAPTER 14

The Perfect Gentleman

I woke up Saturday morning with the same smile J.T. left on my face last night after Jamal's game. I found myself replaying our conversation a hundred times, recounting every word, every expression, every moment. *Slow your roll, Destiny,* I said to myself. With my recent string of bad experiences with men, the last thing I needed was to get all giddy over some tall, incredibly sexy basketball coach who I couldn't seem to get out of my mind...I had to force myself to think about something else, so I turned on some music and kept myself busy by downloading the pictures I had taken of Jamal's game and burning them onto a CD for Walter's aunt.

Around 11:00, I heard the phone ring.

"Hello?"

"Hey, Girl!"

"Miss Lady, how have you been?" I said to Vanessa.

"Blessed. What's up with you?"

"Same old same. Working. Going on bad dates. What about you?"

"Girl, I am so tired. Between work and this master's degree and trying to keep up with Rodney I am about to pull my hair out."

"When have you not had a full plate, Nessa? This is nothing new for you."

"I know. Maybe I'm just getting old." We both laughed.

"Ooh, hold on, Girl. I got a beep." I clicked over to the other line. "Hello?"

"May I speak to Destiny please?" I recognized the thick, deep voice as J.T.'s.

"This is Destiny." I swear he could hear me smiling through the phone.

"This is J.T. I hope you don't mind me calling before noon."

"I don't mind at all. I've been up for awhile. Hold on one second, okay?"

"Sure."

I clicked back over to Vanessa.

"Sweetie, let me call you back. There's a handsome man on the other line who wants to get to know me better."

"Same old same, huh? All right, Girl. Call me later."

"J.T.?" I asked, clicking back over.

"I'm here."

"Sorry about that. I was talking to my friend, Vanessa."

"I didn't mean to interrupt."

"No, don't worry about it. How was the victory celebration?"

"We had a good time as always. I have to admit, I was thinking about you the whole time, though. I really wanted to call you last night, but I held out as long as I could."

Smiles galore. It was nice to know I wasn't the only one thinking about last night.

"What are you doing today?" he asked.

"Hopefully something with you," I said flirtatiously.

"Sounds like music to my ears. We can do anything you want. Just name it."

***

Three hours later, J.T. and I arrived at a seafood restaurant near the Inner Harbor of Baltimore. It turned out that November wasn't the greatest time of year to be close to the water, but it wasn't the cold air that made me shiver; it was the energy beaming from this seemingly flawless man.

J.T. held the door for me as we stepped inside the restaurant and felt the instant warmth of the building. Since we missed the lunch crowd and beat the dinner rush, the hostess immediately sat us at a cozy table in the corner of the room. J.T. pulled out my chair then made sure I was comfortably tucked in before he sat down across from me.

The hostess left us two menus and rattled off the daily special. Then we gave her our drink order and she swiftly disappeared.

"Have you eaten here before?" asked J.T., opening his menu.

"No, I haven't. What's good?"

"I guarantee you'll love anything you could possibly order here. But I'm having the crab legs."

"That sounds good. I think I'll try some, too."

The waitress came back with our drinks, took our crab leg order then vanished once again.

"That's a nice color on you," I said, referring to the cream turtle-neck sweater J.T. was wearing. It was a perfect contrast against his smooth, dark skin. My comment probably sounded as if I was flirting, but it wasn't unusual for me to compliment people when they caught my attention.

"Thanks," he said with a slow smile, as if no one had ever complimented him before. I knew that wasn't true, though. He was gorgeous.

"So," he continued. "Tell me everything about you – everything I don't already know."

"What do you already know about me?" I asked coyly.

"Well, let's see. I know you're a photographer. You have a sister who's dating Jamal's cousin, Walter. You graduated from Chapel Hill. You're left-handed. And you have the most amazing smile I've ever seen."

I blushed.

"How did I do?" he asked.

"Pretty good," I said, showing him every tooth in my mouth. "How did you know I was left-handed?"

He pointed at my glass. "You picked up your drink with your left hand. Lucky guess, though."

I giggled like a little girl.

"So, what made you move to Baltimore?" he asked.

"Well, as you know, my sister lives up here and we're pretty close. We haven't lived in the same state since she left for college, so it's nice being around her again. And it helped that I landed a decent job with a major newspaper."

"You must be pretty talented."

"I guess," I said modestly. "I've loved photography ever since I was a little girl. And when I found out that I could study it in college and do it for a living, I figured it was the perfect job for me."

"I can't remember the last time I took a real picture – of myself or anyone else."

"You should. At least every five years. It's like capturing a piece of history, you know? I always get a kick out of seeing pictures of my parents when they were young. You really never appreciate the value of photos until years after they are taken."

"Where are your parents now?" he asked.

"They live in Richmond." I took a sip of my soda, then asked, "Where is your family?"

"My parents are in Fairfax, Virginia. And I have a younger brother who goes to Princeton. He's a little genius."

"What's his name?"

"Xavier. He's 19 going on 90." We both laughed. "He graduated from high school a year early and now he's a sophomore."

"Impressive."

"He's a smart kid. A good kid, but he's way too high-strung. He's always stressing about grades and the state of the world, which is okay sometimes, but he never takes a break or has any fun. He needs to get himself a girlfriend."

I laughed and admitted, "Girlfriends can be a headache."

"Yeah, but they can balance you, too. I tell him like I tell my students and the guys on my team that life is about balance. Too much of any one thing can throw everything off."

"Right."

"I wish I could get Jamal to understand that. He acts like my brother, but on the opposite extreme. He spends so much time focusing on girls and basketball that he might mess around and not graduate from high school."

"I guess it didn't help that I showed up at the game with my camera like paparazzi."

"No, don't get me wrong. That was sweet of you to do that for Ms. Dunbar. She's good people. I just want my kids to understand how important it is to get an education, especially my black students."

I nodded as he continued. "And Jamal is bright, too. He just doesn't like to turn in his homework. I told him he would have a killer combination if he had skills on the court and the right grades to back him up. But he thinks he can get by on basketball alone."

I listened attentively as J.T. spoke about the high expectations he had for his students and the boys on his team, and how much he wanted them all to succeed. I was completely turned on by his sincerity. He was becoming more and more attractive to me by the minute.

"You're really passionate about your kids, aren't you?"

"Yes, I am. I'm sorry if I've been rambling on."

"I don't mind it at all. It's not everyday when I meet someone with such purpose. You remind me of Vanessa."

I told J.T. about Vanessa's non-profit work and how much I admired her for making things happen in her community. As I was praising my friend, the waitress brought our order, and we situated our napkins and silverware for the occasion. My soul lit up when J.T. clasped my hand and asked God to bless our food.

While dining on our delicious crab legs, we discussed everything from our families, to favorite books, to our opinions of the war. We stayed in the restaurant so long we met the first wave of the dinner crowd.

***

That afternoon, J.T. wired some money to his brother before we continued on our date. We took in a movie and spent the following half hour strolling through the mall exploring random topics that popped into our heads. Our discussion eventually led to the discovery that J.T. had a sweet tooth just like me, so we decided to indulge our craving for some Mrs. Fields cookies. We bought four chocolate chip cookies and two small cartons of milk before settling at a table in the food court and continuing our conversation.

After J.T. finished his chocolate treat he said, "Tell me how someone as smart and beautiful as you doesn't have a special someone in her life."

"I have plenty of special people in my life." I was happy to dodge his query so easily.

"You know what I mean," he said lightly. "A man. A boyfriend."

"I don't know. I guess I'm just waiting for the right one."

"How will you know if you've found the right one?"

I politely swallowed the last bite of my cookie before answering. "I don't know that either. I thought I had found the right one once. But it didn't end up working out. So, I've sort of given up trying to figure this love thing out."

"I hear you. The dating scene can be pretty rough sometimes."

"I could ask the same question about you. Why is it that you're single?" I asked, not even sure if he *was* single.

"I really haven't had a whole lot of time to date lately between teaching and coaching."

I asked innocently enough, "Why did you make time to go on a date with me?"

He slid me a smile. "You just seemed different. Interesting. Worth getting to know better."

J.T opened his hand and stretched it across the table for me to take. I gently placed my hand in his, noticing how strong and smooth it was.

"I'll be honest with you, Destiny. This is the first 'first date' I've had in a long time that I didn't want to end."

He looked into my eyes so intently that I had to glance away for a moment. *What was he trying to do to me?*

When I looked back at him I said, "I'll be right back. I need to run to the ladies' room."

"I'll be here," J.T. said, releasing my hand as I stood up.

I weaved through the tables in the food court and headed toward the women's restroom to handle my business. When I finished, I washed my hands, touched up my lip gloss, and popped a piece of gum into my mouth.

This date is going *really* well, I thought to myself. Too well. J.T.

was handsome, charming, passionate about life, and had the manners of a pure-bred gentleman. But something told me he was too good to be true, and we all know that anything that *seems* too good probably is. I'd have to be careful with this one.

I put a little model swagger in my step as I went back into the food court. But my walk slowed suddenly. Through the Saturday evening mall traffic, I noticed J.T. standing by our table embracing a young woman with shoulder-length curls bouncing as he rocked her back and forth. I all but stopped in my tracks to avoid interrupting their union. The two released their hug and engaged in energetic conversation that had spread a look of exuberance on J.T.'s face. So as not to look like a stalker myself, I turned away from them and headed to the nearest restaurant counter to order some water.

The three minutes it took to stand in line and get my water happened way too fast. I hesitated to look back at the table, but when I did, J.T. caught my gaze and beckoned me to come to him. As I made my way back to the table, I took in a better view of the young lady who had made J.T. smile wider than he had the whole night. Caramel skin, red lips, petite figure, stylish outfit, arm *still* around my date.

J.T. smiled at my return.

"I'm back!" I said, over-compensating for how awkward I felt.

"Destiny, I want you to meet Alicia. She's one of my first math students at Mercer who graduated two years ago," said J.T. proudly.

I reached out to shake her hand. "How nice to meet you! I'm Destiny."

"Nice to meet you," Alicia said with her red-lipped smiled.

J.T. continued. "Alicia's a sophomore at Howard University now and she's majoring in accounting. She was one of my best and brightest students."

"Oh, Mr. Walker," Alicia said bashfully. "I was only a good student because you were such a good teacher." She turned to me and winked. "And it didn't hurt that he was so attractive. Every girl in the school had a crush on Mr. Walker. But he was always the perfect gentleman. He gave me hope that I could find a good man like him someday."

Not today, sister! said an evil voice from my subconscious. All I could do was smile.

"I'd better let you two get back to your date. It was so good to see you again, Mr. Walker." Alicia gave J.T. a final hug. "And it was nice to meet you, Destiny."

"Take care. And good luck in school," I said to her.

"Thanks."

Alicia went off to join her friends at another table as J.T. and I sat back down at ours.

"She seems like a sweet girl," I said, undeniably relieved at the innocence of the situation.

"She is. I'm glad to see she's doing so well. Seasoned teachers always tell me the most rewarding part of our job is running into a student you had an impact on. It may not happen very often, but when it does, it feels great."

Too good to be true, I thought to myself.

"Have you ever been Salsa dancing?" J.T. asked, suddenly changing the subject.

"No, I haven't," I said, excited by the thought that our date wasn't nearing the end.

"Wanna go tonight?"

"Is that where you take all your first dates?" I asked.

Underneath his beautiful brown skin I swore he was blushing.

"Only the special ones," he said with a smile.

The rest of the evening was nothing short of exhilarating. J.T. and I went back to our respective homes and changed clothes before he took me to a salsa club. We danced, and laughed and held hands like we had known each other for ages. It was the most fun I had had since I moved to my new city.

It was one-thirty in the morning when J.T. walked me to the front door of Angel's condo. My feet were sore from hours of pretending I knew how to salsa; but I wouldn't have traded the feeling for anything in the world.

J.T. stood in front of me, shielding me from the wind when he asked, "What are your plans for tomorrow, or should I say later on today?"

"I'll probably go to church around eleven. But other than that, nothing special."

J.T. grew quiet and studied my face.

"You are so beautiful," he said finally. His words truly made me feel that way.

"And you are such a gentleman, J.T. Thank you for showing me a great time."

"Anytime, Sweetheart." He wrapped his arms around me and placed a tender kiss on my forehead.

"Well, I'm gonna let you get some rest. I'll give you a call soon, okay?" he said, stepping back from our embrace.

"All right," I said sweetly.

"Goodnight."

I watched J.T. make his way to his car and drive away. The whole night felt like a dream.

***

"Shutterbug." Angel knocked on my bedroom door as she opened it. "Are you going to church this morning?"

I groaned and stretched my tired limbs under the covers, half asleep.

"Yeah."

"Well, say a prayer for me because I have to go into the office today. How was your date?"

"Good," I moaned.

"I want details later. You better get up now if you're going to church."

I got dressed, ate a small breakfast then grabbed my coat, keys and Bible before heading out the door. A brisk breeze and a splash of sunlight welcomed me into the world. It was a cold, but gorgeous mid-autumn day.

As I was about to open my car door, I was pleasantly surprised to see J.T. pulling his car into a parking space near mine. I beamed as I waited for him to get out of his car, and when he did, I beamed even more. He was wearing a dress shirt, a tie, and slacks with a jacket, looking like something out of GQ magazine.

"Good morning, Sunshine," he said as he stepped onto the sidewalk near my car.

"Good morning! What brings you by?"

"Time to go to church, right? I thought you might like a ride."

"You want to go to church with me?" I asked, surprised.

"Sure. Come on." He took me by the hand and escorted me to his car.

"You are something else," I said to J.T. as we drove to the church.

"What do you mean?"

"You have made me smile more in the past twenty-four hours than I have in the past six months. And I don't even really know you."

"I'm just doing my job, ma'am. What street do I need to turn on?"

"Lincoln Avenue."

J.T. made the turn.

"Do you normally go to church?" I asked.

It was a question I'd been dying to ask him ever since I got in the car. I hesitated to find out because I didn't want to accuse him of going to church just to impress me, but I needed to know if that was the case.

"Not as much as I should. I get a little lazy sometimes, but I know it's where I need to be on Sundays." He gave me a cute, crooked smile. "My mother didn't play when it came to me and my brother going to church. I didn't like it when I was a kid, but I thank her for it now."

"Why is that?" I asked, curiously.

"I don't know. I guess some people spend most of their lives searching for the truth about life. If you're introduced to Christ as a kid, at least you have some place to start."

"That's an interesting way to look at it."

"How do you look at it?" he asked.

I glanced over at J.T. "Do you really want to know?"

"I want to know everything about you," he said.

I cleared my throat and thought about how to answer his question. "Well, I've believed in God ever since I was eight years old, and I received Christ when I was 12."

"Wow."

"Yeah. I know it sounds crazy, but I actually remember it to the day. I was playing with my Barbie dolls while my mom was cleaning the house and listening to this gospel album, right. I don't know the name of the song, but I remember that the words made me cry. It was as if God was telling me that He loved me and I was special to Him, you know? It was such a peace I felt that day, and ever since, I have never questioned His existence."

When I finished my brief recollection, J.T. remained speechless. I hoped I hadn't scared him into thinking I was a Jesus-Freak or something. I just felt so comfortable talking to him.

"I can see Him in you, Destiny."

I smiled and shook my head in astonishment.

"That's the nicest thing anyone has ever said to me."

"I'm serious. I could tell from the first moment I saw you that you were special. Women like you don't come along everyday. And believe me, I've been looking."

"What have you been looking for?"

I couldn't help but notice how cute he looked driving with a left-handed lean.

J.T. sighed before answering. "I guess I'm looking for someone I can trust with everything. Someone I can spoil without feeling like she might take advantage of me, you know what I'm saying?"

"Yeah."

"Some women won't have anything to do with you unless you dress a certain way, drive a certain car and make a certain amount of money. It's hard to trust someone like that."

"Trust is a big deal," I added.

"Yes it is."

"What other qualities are you looking for?" I queried.

"I want someone who values family, who enjoys life and is thankful for it. I want someone who is positive, outgoing; confident, but humble. Someone who will challenge me mentally and spiritually, and who will make me want to be a better person."

"I can tell you've given this some thought," I said, amused.

"Haven't we all? Tell me what you're looking for."

"I'm not looking for anything right now. The moment I start looking for something I'll end up finding exactly what I don't want," I said, hoping it didn't sound like I was bitter.

"But what's your *ideal* relationship?"

"Hmmmm. I want to be in a relationship where I can feel free to love with my whole heart and not hold anything back. No liars or cheaters. I want someone who will support my dreams and inspire me to reach them. And I definitely need someone who is led by God and will encourage my spiritual growth." I huffed. "That seems like a lot to ask for, doesn't it?"

"That's not a lot to ask for," he said. "It's what you deserve."

Just then J.T. pulled into the church parking lot. I loved where our conversation was going and I didn't want it to end, but we got out of the car and went inside to enjoy the service. After church, we went out to lunch then J.T. took me back to the condo. I invited him to come inside so we could talk some more.

The thrill in Angel's eyes was glaringly obvious when she came home from the office and saw J.T. and I sitting next to each other on the couch. She had been trying to get me in the company of a man ever since I moved in with her, and I could tell she was happy I had found someone to hold my interest. Angel greeted my guest then went upstairs to her bedroom so J.T. and I could continue our 'getting-to-know-you' session.

J.T. must've noticed the photo album wedged between books on the book shelf in the corner because he asked, "Have we known each other long enough for me to see pictures of you and your family?"

"Sure we have," I said, easing off the couch. "You are so observant. Is there anything you don't notice?"

"Nothing," he said matter-of-factly.

I retrieved the family photo album and brought it to J.T. who opened it eagerly. I sat down next to him so I could explain the whos and whats of each photo. As we flipped through the album together, I leaned into his space a little more than necessary, enchanted by his cologne. Everything about him was magnetic.

"Look at baby Destiny," he mocked as he came across a picture of me as an infant. "Destiny Phillips," he said probingly. "What's your middle name?"

"I don't have one. I have a nickname, though. It's stupid, but my whole family calls me 'Shutterbug.'"

"Shutterbug?" J.T. let out a deep, throaty laugh. "That's cute. Why do they call you that?"

"Because *I* was cute!" I said, being silly. "But, seriously, it's what they call people who are fanatical about photography. It's even in the dictionary."

"All right, Shutterbug." He laughed again.

"Ha, ha. Anyway, I know your first name is Julius, but what does the 'T' stand for?"

"My middle name," he joked.

"It must be a good one if you're shy about it."

"It's Terrell. Actually most of my family calls me by that name. Anything is better than Julius."

"Well, Terrell, or J.T., Coach Walker, or whatever, I just want you to know that you have made this a wonderful weekend for me. Even if I never see you again, I feel like I'm a better person for having met you."

"I hope that doesn't mean you don't want to see me again."

"Of course I want to see you again," I said definitively.

J.T. took my hand and kissed it. "I better get going, though," he said. "I have a load of tests to grade before tomorrow."

"Okay, I'll walk you out."

I followed J.T. to the door, subconsciously hoping he might attempt to kiss me. But instead he gave me a tender bear hug and his patented forehead kiss. He told me he would call me soon, then I watched him walk to his car and drive off.

As soon as J.T. was out of sight, I scrambled to my bedroom to call Vanessa. She needed to hear every detail of the incredible weekend I'd just had.

Serena K. Wallace

CHAPTER 15

Skinnin' & Grinnin' Like A Cat

I was on a natural high the rest of the week. I had a little bop in my step and I found myself singing aloud in the shower and on my way to work. And I owed it all to my newfound friend named Julius Terrell Walker. The Monday following our first date, J.T. set the tone for my week by sending me flowers at work.

The card attached read, "Dear Shutterbug, I hope your day is as beautiful as you are. Signed, Not-a-Stalker."

I smiled as wide as the ocean as I smelled the array of fresh flowers and read the card over and over again. *Be careful, Destiny,* my brain told me. *Don't fall for this guy too fast.* But my heart was not paying attention. I tried to allow myself to enjoy being wooed by a handsome man - while it lasted, anyway. My common sense reminded me that Damian used to make me feel special like this.

"Well, aren't those lovely," said Aileen, as she came into the office and invited herself to smell my flowers. "I see things are looking up!"

I gave her a closed-lip smile that warned her not to pry. She got the hint.

Just then the phone rang and Aileen picked it up.

"Photo department," she answered. "Yes, hold one moment please." She held out the phone to me. "It's for you, Destiny."

"Thank you." I said, very business-like and took the phone from her.

"Hello?"

"Good. I'm glad you're there. Do you have any breaks between assignments today?" I recognized Angel's voice on the other end.

"Ahhh, yeah. Probably after lunch. Why?"

"I want you to meet me on North May Avenue at one o'clock. I think I've found an office building for the firm!"

After I shot my morning assignments and grabbed a bite to eat, I drove to the office building where Angel wanted me to meet her that afternoon. I spotted her car and parked next to it before heading toward the red brick building. The marquee outside of the entrance listed the names of several businesses including a tax and title service, a mortgage company, an insurance company, even the office of a speech therapist. One of the listings read "Office Space for Lease."

I stepped inside the front door and searched for any sign of Angel, and moments later, she poked her head out of one of the glass office doors and waved me in her direction. I joined her in the office and found Angel engaged in light conversation with a stocky, older black gentleman with graying hair and a sharp suit.

"D, I'm glad you could make it! This is my real estate agent, Sam Porter. Sam, this is my sister, Destiny," Angel introduced. I shook Sam's hand.

"Good to meet you," said Sam in a husky voice. "I'll leave you two alone to look the place over while I return a phone call," he said, then quickly exited the office.

"Isn't it perfect!" Angel exclaimed. "It's just the right size! And with a fresh coat of paint and some updated carpet, it'll be gorgeous!"

"I like it. And it's not too far from home," I noted as I walked around and observed the layout.

The place was well-lit and had a large executive office with a window, plenty of room for a reception area and a separate space that could easily be turned into a mini-conference room.

Angel glowed with excitement.

"Shutter, I've been praying about this for a long time," she said. "I didn't want to move until God said move, and it's time. And I know this is the place!"

Her voice cracked as she spoke and her eyes began to glisten. I went to my big sister and wrapped my arms around her polished business suit and squeezed her tightly in a hug. It was the first time I'd seen her cry since we were kids.

Angel was the strong one. Angel was the smart one. Angel was the pretty one. Everything I envied about her as a little girl made me so proud of her as a grown woman. I could only hope to be as amazing as she was.

"Look at me getting all emotional," she said releasing our hug. "You better get back to work. I just wanted you to see it before I sign the lease."

"It's beautiful, Sis."

"Yeah. I'll have to be extra sweet to Walter this week," Angel said, dabbing her eyes with a tissue. "He's the one who helped me find it and get hooked up with Sam."

"What a wonderful boyfriend!" I said teasingly.

"Yes, he is. And he speaks highly of *your* new friend. How are things going with J.T.?"

Ear to ear smile. "He had flowers sent to my office this morning!" I said, giddily.

"Ooooh, flowers. You better watch out, Shutter. He just might be The One."

"You think any man who pays me attention could be The One," I joked. "Besides, I've only known him for four days."

"And he already has you skinnin' and grinnin' like a cat!"

We both laughed out loud.

***

That night when I got home from work, I called J.T. at his apartment to thank him for the flowers. I tried to wait until eight o'clock when I knew he would be home from basketball practice.

"Hello?" J.T. answered.

"Hello, Mister Not-a-Stalker," I said in a mischievous voice. "I just wanted to thank you for the flowers."

"My pleasure, Sweetheart. How was your day?" J.T. asked. He sounded sweet, but tired.

"It was great. How about yours?"

"Long and busy. But better now that I hear your voice."

"You sound so tired."

"I am a little. I hit the gym after practice today and I've been up since five."

"That *is* a long day," I said.

"Yeah, I've got a lot on my plate this week, but I'd love to see you again. What are your plans for the weekend?"

"No plans so far."

"Let's meet up on Saturday. We can do anything you want."

"Anything?" I asked.

"Anything."

I guarantee this wasn't what J.T. had in mind when he said that we could do *anything* I wanted. I dragged him into the 37-degree weather that Saturday to take pictures at a city park. Bundled up in our winter coats, we were two of very few people crazy enough to be outside. I shot pictures of J.T. in all types of poses, from sitting in a swing to talking to a disheveled old man who was ambling throughout the park.

"I guess I never should've told you how long it's been since I've taken a photo, huh?" said J.T. in good sport. Now he was leaning against a tree, striking an exaggerated model pose.

"Guess not. Now bring your shoulder toward me and give me that sexy smile," I taunted.

J.T. reluctantly struck another pose just as a gust of wind blew by. "I am not the modeling kind of guy, Destiny. I must *really* like you."

"I wish you could see what I see, Handsome," I said, feeling flirty. "The camera loves you."

He laughed just then, and I caught it on camera.

"All right, I think we've taken enough," he said bashfully. "Show me how to use this thing so I can get some pictures of *you*." He came toward me and tried to confiscate my camera.

"No, no, no," I said, playfully backing away. "Today is *your* photo shoot!"

"Pleeeeeeease!" he begged, adorably.

"Maybe some other time when I'm not looking like Medusa. This wind is something terrible!"

"You look perfect. Let me see this."

I relented and let J.T take my 35mm camera after I gave him a brief lesson on how to use it. Once he had snapped seven or eight shots of me and my wind-blown hair, the roll of film was all used up.

"Too bad, so sad," I said in a childish rhyme. I retrieved my camera from the amateur and placed it back in its case. "I suppose I've tortured you enough for one day. What do you want to do next?"

J.T. wrapped his arm around me as we walked back to his car. "I say we get out of the cold and get something to eat."

"I can get with that," I agreed.

We nestled into a table at a local delicatessen and ordered a late lunch. As we waited for our food, J.T. thawed my hands by placing them between his and blowing warm air onto them. The texture of his lips against the delicate skin on my hand made me wonder how it would feel to kiss him. *Calm down, Destiny*, I told myself.

"What's going on in that mind of yours?" J.T. asked thoughtfully. Nothing gets past this guy!

"I'm just enjoying your company. I must say you are a welcomed surprise. I wasn't expecting to meet someone like you."

"What do you mean?" he asked, with a soft smile, caressing my hands with his fingertips.

"You're just very different from any man I've met in my short lifetime. Everyone thinks so much of you. You're a gentleman. You're so attractive and intelligent…God-fearing. I just can't seem to find anything wrong with you."

"I have my flaws just like everyone else," he said humbly.

"Well, you sure do a great job at hiding them. What kind of flaws are you masking so well?"

"I can't tell you that! It would ruin all the mystery," he laughed. "Seriously, though. My list of imperfections is probably just as long as the next guy."

"Name some," I dared.

"Let me see." J.T. looked deep in thought. "Well, I snore and I have bad breath in the morning. I'm a chronic channel surfer - oh, and the big one! I leave the toilet seat up at my apartment."

We both laughed.

"That's not too bad," I said, still chuckling.

Moments later, the waitress brought us our sandwiches then J.T. thanked God for our food.

"So, tell me where you see yourself in ten years?" J.T. asked between bites of food.

Thankfully, he abandoned our conversation about imperfections. He was right. It might ruin all the mystery.

"I'm not sure. I've always hated that question because I sort of go where I'm led, you know. I mean, I have things I want to achieve, but they don't have to happen in any certain order."

"What sort of things?" J.T. inquired.

"Things like owning my photography studio one day. Most photographers either love photojournalism or still-photography, but I love them both. I'd really like to buy a house and open the studio there. That way I could have a flexible work schedule and spend time with my husband and kids."

"So you want a family?"

"Oh, yeah," I said emphatically. "I've always wanted a family. But first things first, right? I've got to find the right man."

"First things first," J.T. agreed.

"What about you? Where do *you* see yourself in ten years?"

"Man! In ten years I'll be *thirty-five*," he said with an exaggerated hint of dread. "By then I plan to have my master's degree in education administration and be a high school principal somewhere here in Maryland. I'd like to have a house, a family, and be well on my way to having enough money in the bank to send my kids to any college of their choice."

I was impressed. "That sounds like a good plan. But I still don't get it," I said.

"Don't get what?"

"How you could be so…" *Perfect for me!* I wanted to say. But my good sense took over. "So, single."

"I don't mean to sound conceited, Destiny. But I'm very picky about who I choose to have in my life. I believe God helps me discern who I should invest time in and who I should keep at a distance."

I hesitated, but I had to know. "What did He say about me?"

"He said you were a whole lot of trouble and I needed to stay as far away from you as possible."

Not quite the sincere and romantic comment I was expecting.

"I'm joking, Sweetheart," said J.T., his facial expression suddenly becoming reverent. "I wouldn't be here with you now if I wasn't supposed to be."

***

"Nessa, I am in so much trouble," I said to my friend on the phone. I had just gotten home from another date with J.T. that had left me in seventh heaven.

"What are you talking about? He sounds like a good catch to me. Almost unbelievable," Vanessa said.

"I know. He's…really something. I love spending time with him, and I feel like I can truly be myself when he's around."

"So what's the problem?"

"What if I take a chance on this guy and he lets me down? I don't think I can take another heart break. Ever again."

"I don't know what to tell you, D. You're the only one who knows if you're ready to start a new relationship."

"Yeah, I know. It feels good to have someone in my life that makes me so happy, but I'm scared to death! I don't want to spend all my time worrying about everything that could go wrong," I whined. "Maybe I'm not in the best shape to be with someone new. I *really* like him, though."

"You know my advice is going to be the same as it always is. Pray about it."

"I will. That's your advice for everything, huh?"

"Everything that matters," she said matter-of-factly.

"That's why I love you, Girl. You're always giving sound advice."

When I got off the phone with Vanessa, I decided to take her advice immediately. I flopped onto my bed, slid to my knees and closed my eyes.

"Dear, Lord," I prayed. "Thank you for allowing me to see this day that was not promised to me. Thank you for the blessings I did not deserve. Thank you for hearing my prayer today. You know my only desire is to live a life that is pleasing in your sight. So I ask you for your divine wisdom about my relationship with J.T. If he is someone you have placed in my life, let him fulfill his purpose, and nothing more. If he is someone I need to rid from my life, please give me the strength to do so." A tear fell from my eye and I continued. "Lord, I know you know what's best for me. You know my heart. You know my pain. Please heal this wound so I can be free to love again without fear. I trust you and I love you, Lord. Amen."

CHAPTER 16

The Cave

"Hey, Coach Walker! I think you have a visitor," yelled a tall, lanky, brown boy in a sweaty t-shirt and shorts three times too big for his scrawny behind.

He and the other members of the Mercer basketball team paused from their frantic drill on the court and beamed their eyes in my direction as I entered the musty-smelling gym. I smiled and waved at them like an adoring fan, wondering how they knew I was there for "Coach Walker."

J.T. gave me a quick wink before finishing his conversation with Coach Maze on the opposite side of the gym. That trademark wink eased my apprehension about showing up at his school unannounced. No way was I going to be accused of being the stalker after I had teased J.T. about it. Thankfully, he looked genuinely happy to see me. We had only been dating for a month and I didn't want him to feel smothered already.

I took a seat on one of the bleachers pulled out from the gym wall and entertained myself by watching the guys run plays on the court. Moments later, my eyes shifted toward J.T. as he coolly made his way over to me, his chest and abdominal muscles outlined under the stretch of his t-shirt. *Lord, help me.*

"Hey, Gorgeous," he said, popping a sweet kiss on my cheek then sitting down at my side.

"Hey, how was your day?"

"It's perfect now that I get to see you."

"You're so sweet. I hope you don't mind me coming to practice. I just wanted to lay eyes on you for a few minutes before my next assignment."

"Working pretty late again?"

"Yeah."

"What about this weekend?"

"I'm off this weekend," I said, in hopeful anticipation of spending more time with J.T.

"Good. I want to take you out if you don't have any plans. There's this spot called The Cave where my boy Chris and his jazz band are playing this Saturday. A couple of my other friends will be there, too, and I want you to meet them."

"Sounds like fun. Just tell me when and I'll be ready."

"How about eight o'clock. I'll pick you up and we can grab some dinner before we go."

"It's a date then," I said, patting J.T.'s leg. "I'd better let you get back to your team. I didn't come to distract you."

"Believe me. You are a welcome distraction."

J.T. gave me another quick kiss on the cheek before he rose from his seat and headed toward the center of the court. I felt my face getting warm at the sight of his buns-of-steel thundering with each step he took. Then it got even warmer with embarrassment when one of his players caught me watching. *Mental note. No more visits during basketball practice.*

***

"You really like this guy, don't you?" Angel asked, reclining on my bed and watching me get dressed for my date. I was fumbling with the strap on my pumps because my hands were shaking just enough to make me miss the hole. Apparently, I was a little uptight about meeting J.T.'s friends for the first time. I knew they were important to him and I wanted to make a good impression.

"Yeah, I do. I like him a lot," I responded. I had finally fastened my strap and was now searching for earrings in my jewelry box. "I know I may sound naïve because I've only known J.T. for a few weeks, but there is something special about him. I can't put my finger on what it is. He's just such a…"

"Such a what?" Angel urged with a grin.

"A *man*!" I said as I turned around to face her, excited and dramatic. "I don't know. He's such a man, Angel, and he makes me feel like a woman. Does that sound stupid?"

"Not at all," she assured.

"When I say he makes me feel like a woman I don't mean in the sexual sense – even though he *is* fine."

"Amen."

"He makes me feel cherished and precious, you know? Maybe I'm just crazy. Maybe I haven't been treated well in so long that I'm making a bigger deal out of this than necessary. But, I definitely like him."

"I'm happy for you, Baby Sis," Angel supported. "It's about time you started having some fun."

J.T. picked me up at eight-o-clock sharp, looking as delicious as chocolate cake with extra ice cream. His deep, navy blue suit fit him to perfection and he wore his collar open with no tie. He greeted me with a tender hug as he entered the condo, making my heart flutter like butterfly wings.

"You are simply gorgeous," he said persuasively, as we released our embrace.

He spun me around and admired the jazzy red dress Angel and I had picked out just for the occasion.

Obviously down-playing how absolutely scrumptious he looked, I said, "You're not too hard to look at yourself."

"Turn around, you two. Let me take your picture," said Angel, holding a small, digital camera. There must've been a little shutterbug in her, too.

"Angel, we're not going to the prom," I whined.

"I know, but you look so good. Come on. Smile for me."

You had to love her.

After our mini photo session, J.T. and I had an intimate dinner at a restaurant before we met J.T.'s friends at a nightclub called The Cave where his friend's band was performing. Our dinner had taken a little longer than expected, so when we arrived, the band had already begun to play.

A sultry, female voice flowing from the stage greeted us in song as we entered a room lit only with miniature lamps on each round table covered in white cloth. The club was dark and eclectic, purposely designed to look like a cave with jazz mosaics and paintings on the walls. The loud, soulful music carried us through the club as we found J.T.'s friends sitting at a table for six. One of his friends roared in approval of J.T.'s presence and stood up to give him a brotherly hug.

"What's up, Man! I haven't seen you in weeks. This must be the young lady who's been occupying all your time," said J.T.'s friend, with an infectious smile.

"Destiny, this is my boy, Tony."

"Nice to meet you, Tony," I said, shaking his hand.

"Likewise," Tony responded.

Tony took it upon himself to be the official introducer. "Everyone, this is J.T.'s lady-friend, Destiny."

The group politely waved at me.

"Destiny, this here is my lovely date, Michelle. This is Andre and his date, Vonda. And this is Chris's wife, Yvette. Chris is up there on stage." He pointed. "The yellow brother playing guitar."

"Nice to meet you all," I said.

I was suddenly distracted when I recognized the name and face of the gentleman introduced to me as Andre. I couldn't quite remember where I knew him from, but I had definitely seen his face before. *My* face, however, obviously didn't ring a bell because he pleasantly treated me like a perfect stranger.

"We need to get another chair over here," said Tony, scanning the club and noticing that no other chairs were available.

"Don't worry about it, man. She can sit with me," J.T. decided.

He took a seat in the last open chair at the table then gently guided my hips into his lap. I crossed my legs and wrapped an arm around his neck, trying to settle comfortably into my make-shift chair. I felt a little awkward, towering above everyone at the table. It was nice being near J.T., though. He held me close and carefully like I belonged to him. And I liked it.

The gathering of friends swapped inside jokes and we all laughed at the antics of Tony, who I quickly observed was the comedian of the group. I found myself feeling at ease in the company of J.T.'s high-spirited friends. But what I enjoyed most was the sound of J.T.'s laughter. It was deep and resounding, and it made me happy to see him happy.

Chris's band played until midnight then a D.J. began to play a mix of dance music. As heavy Hip Hop beats spread throughout the club, people began to swarm the dance floor off to the side of the stage. Tony, Andre and their dates quickly followed the crowd, while Chris's wife went to find her husband. J.T. and I were left alone at the table, sitting inches apart from each other, now in separate chairs.

"You having a good time?" asked J.T., winding his arm around my waist.

"I always have a good time when I'm with you," I said sweetly. I snuggled closer to him.

Just then, we both glanced across the room to the dance floor and caught sight of Tony and Michelle dancing wild enough to draw a crowd.

"My friends are so crazy," said J.T. in awe.

"A little," I joked. "But they're a lot of fun. They seem to make you happy."

"*You* make me happy," he said, turning to gaze into my eyes. He clasped my hand and kissed the back of it. "I noticed the expression on your face when you saw Andre again. Did you remember him from that night at Jasper's?"

"Jasper's?" I asked, crinkling my forehead. "The restaurant? How did you know about that?"

"I was there. We messed with Andre for going over to talk to you since it was obvious you were waiting for your date."

"I remember him now! Why didn't you tell me about this before?" I asked, feigning more embarrassment than I really felt.

"There was really no easy way to tell you. I didn't want you to feel awkward about meeting my friends before you got here. And Andre didn't want to embarrass his date, so he said he would just pretend the whole thing never happened."

"Probably a good idea. Well, at least I know where I remember his face from. I remember that night…and that awful date."

J.T. laughed out loud. "I had a feeling there wouldn't be a second date when I saw the two of you sitting there. You looked as bored as I don't know what."

"So, you're saying you were stalking me?" I ribbed.

"Of course not, Sweetheart. I told you that's not my style. I'm just a people-watcher. There's a difference," he said with a half-smile. "I just couldn't help but notice a change in the atmosphere when you stepped into the room that night. I couldn't take my eyes of you."

"Sounds like a stalker to me," I teased.

J.T. leaned toward me, his lips just inches away from my face.

"When I saw you that night, something inside told me that I would see you again. You looked so beautiful and innocent. I just wanted to know your name. And when I saw you again at the game, I was like, 'this has got to be fate.'"

I smiled and batted my eyes slowly as he spoke.

"I am so crazy about you, Destiny."

"I'm crazy about you, too," I whispered.

"No, I really need you to understand me, Sweetheart." J.T. had a serious look on his face that I had never seen before.

"I don't think you know how open I am right now," he continued. "I'm not usually like this. I don't open up to people like I have with you. I don't trust people like I trust you. You are so…sweet and genuine. I just want to take care of you and make you laugh, make you smile."

If any other man had said that to me, I would've laughed and wrote it off as a line. But I believed J.T. Maybe I was just a sucker for punishment. It was probably too soon to be falling in love again after I had been hurt so badly. But I felt myself falling, and I didn't want to stop.

"Tell me what you're thinking," he said attentively.

I took a quick breath and smiled. "I'm thinking that I could get used to this."

"Get used to what?" he asked.

"Being happy."

"I'll do whatever I can to keep you feeling this way, Love."

He leaned into me and rested his warm, pillow-soft lips on mine. The world stopped for that one moment. It was a single, tender kiss with the promise of many more to come. But it was all I needed to confirm what my heart already knew.

Chapter 17

Old Stuff

It was official. Brick by brick, J.T. was beginning to tear down the wall I had built around my heart. Unfortunately, the demolition was halted by an unwanted message on my voicemail one afternoon.

"Destiny, this is Damian," he said in a slow, quiet voice. "I ah. I just wanted to see how you're doing and everything. I know you said not to call, but I had to hear your voice. Call me, okay? Please. I just want to talk."

I guess Damian sensed that I was really moving on without him, so he decided to call and disrupt my peace. As usual, my stomach twisted and turned at the sound of his voice. He really knew how to ruin my day. But I snapped myself out of it and decided that today would be different. I was happy without him and I wasn't going to let him suck me back into his drama. I deleted his message and went about my business.

Throughout the next few weeks J.T. became an unofficial regular in my life. We had gotten so close so fast that I couldn't even remember what my life was like before I met him. We spent almost all of our down-time together, working out at the gym, watching movies, taking salsa-dancing lessons, and going to church on Sundays.

During the course of our courtship, J.T. and I discovered our new favorite pastime - kissing. One afternoon, we were supposed to be watching a rented version of Denzel Washington's latest masterpiece at J.T.'s apartment, but instead we found ourselves stretched out on his couch exploring each other's mouths.

I've always wondered why kissing felt so good. And why it always made you feel like doing more than kissing, but J.T. and I agreed that we wanted nothing but the best for our relationship, which meant that it had to be honored by God, which meant we couldn't mess things up with pre-marital sex.

I'll shamefully admit that we might have fallen from grace a time or two if it weren't for J.T.'s restraint. Sometimes my will power failed to show up in a moment of weakness, but it made me realize how important it was to be in a relationship in which both people placed the spiritual needs of the other above their own physical needs. That day, I guess it was my turn to be weak.

"Maybe we should stop," said J.T., breathless from our session of affection. As I laid there, panting, pinioned under his powerful body, unable to do anything but look into his eyes. He graced me with another round of soul-stirring kisses before he eased off of me and stood to his feet. "I'll be right back," he said, then moved swiftly to the bathroom to calm down.

I took in a deep breath and tried to re-compose myself, smoothing out my hair and clothes as I waited for J.T. to return. I smiled to myself thinking about what a treasure I'd found. I was beginning to think it was impossible to find a handsome Christian man who could make my heart sing, but I had found one. The only problem was going to be keeping myself from tearing off his clothes all the time. I was going to need the Lord's help on that one.

I let my eyes roam J.T.'s surprisingly clean and well-decorated bachelor pad. He had a comfortable brown leather sofa and a love seat accented with deep colors and exotic prints. His entertainment center was stocked with top-of-the-line equipment, and his abundant CD collection was neatly organized into decorative racks in the corner. To top it all off, he kept a spotless kitchen, which was more than I could say for me and Angel.

While admiring my surroundings, I noticed that J.T.'s wooden coffee table in front of the couch looked as if it could be opened. Almost instinctively, I removed the magazines and miscellaneous pieces of mail off the table and tested my hunch. The solid wood panel slid open and I discovered a small stack of photos tucked inside the table.

I grinned ear to ear as each photo painted a more vibrant picture of J.T.'s life in my mind. One picture captured J.T. and I assumed, his brother straddling bikes that looked too big for them to ride. There was a photo of J.T. posing in his high school basketball uniform, and another of him wearing a graduation cap and gown. Then I flipped through some pictures of family members and friends who I didn't recognize. *Who is this?* I stopped short when one of the unrecognizable people was a beautiful, young woman leaning against J.T.'s car.

I studied the photo intently, drowning out anything that didn't have to do with deciphering who this woman was. I silently hoped it was his cousin or something, but my common sense told me she was a former girlfriend. Against my temperate nature, an ugly twinge of jealously emerged from the pit of my stomach. I must've known that a wonderful, devastatingly handsome man like J.T. had past relationships, but I didn't like seeing the face of woman he had probably kissed, or possibly even loved.

Before I had time to register my feelings, I heard J.T. open the bathroom door. A flash of guilt flowed through me as I scrambled to put the photos away, but I only had enough time to put the picture of the girl on the bottom of the stack before J.T. came back in the living room and sat down next to me.

"You caught me red-handed," I said self-consciously, praying I wouldn't lose points with him for being nosy.

"That's all right, Snoopy. I came to your place and looked through your photos, so I guess it's your turn to get in some laughs."

I gave him a fake chuckle.

J.T. reminisced and shared stories as he walked me through each photo, pointing out all the people I didn't know.

When we got to the picture of the pretty girl, he said, "That's enough of that boring stuff. You want to start the movie over?"

I huffed at his horrible attempt to brush off the last photo.

"Who's this?" I asked as innocently as possible, flashing the photo of the mystery woman.

He tried to ease the photo from my hand.

"That's just…That's an old picture."

"She's standing in front of the car that you bought last year. How old could the picture be?" I asked as I moved the photo from his grasp.

I was beginning to sound like a jealous girlfriend. Maybe I was.

"Let's not talk about that right now. I'm gonna start the movie over."

"You don't feel comfortable talking about her?"

"Why would I be uncomfortable?" he asked, obviously uncomfortable.

"Is she an ex-girlfriend?"

"Yeah. But I'm sure you don't want to talk about old stuff."

"Sure I do. Let's talk about 'old stuff'," I said sarcastically.

J.T.'s face turned solemn. "I'd rather not, Destiny. Let's just watch the movie."

Every ounce of fun we were having was instantly sucked out of the room. While I stacked the photos back into the table and arranged things the way they were before I meddled, J.T. reached for the DVD remote control and started the movie from the beginning. He put his arm around me and scooted me toward him.

Arms crossed, I sat next to him sulking like a spoiled brat, but not really knowing why. Millions of questions swirled in my mind about this nameless woman who J.T. loved or hated so much he couldn't even talk about her. I had found a subject J.T. wasn't willing to discuss and it annoyed me. It annoyed me so much that the childish feeling that causes temper tantrums began to surface, and I wanted to go home.

"I think I'm gonna go home and take care of a few things. Let me know how the movie turns out," I said, slowly raising myself off the couch.

J.T. reached up and took my hand. "What's wrong, Sweetheart? Are you feeling okay?"

"Yeah, I just have some stuff to do," I pouted.

Pulling away from his gentle grasp, I retrieved my coat from the hall closet and slipped my arms in.

"Destiny, are you serious? You're not mad are you?"

"Mad about what?"

"You want to talk about it, don't you?"

"What? What are you talking about?" I asked, playing dumb.

"Shayla. My relationship with her."

The girl had a name. And I didn't like him saying it. Maybe I *didn't* want to talk about it.

"J.T., we don't have to."

"How about you go first," he suggested, as he turned off the television with the remote. He turned his whole body on the couch to face me. "Tell me about your past relationships."

"There was nobody before you," I joked, trying to lighten the mood.

"I'm serious. We're gonna have to talk about it eventually. So, tell me."

"What do you want to know?" I asked, humoring him.

"Your last boyfriend. What was his name?"

The conversation had definitely turned serious. All smiles had disappeared from J.T.'s face.

"Damian," I said reluctantly.

"Tell me about him," he rushed.

"Maybe this wasn't such a good idea."

"Why not?"

"Why are you acting like this?" I asked, my feelings a little hurt by his curtness.

"I'm not acting like anything. You wanted to talk about it so let's talk."

I averted my eyes from J.T.'s intense gaze; sorry I had ever opened Pandora's Box.

"I'm just gonna go, okay. I'll give you a call later."

Before I could blink, I was standing outside in the cold air. I walked to my car a little slower than usual because I honestly expected J.T. to come after me, and I didn't want him to have to run too fast or too far. But he never came. I sat in my car for a few moments before I drove home wondering, *what did I just do?*

***

Words could not describe how utterly deranged I felt driving home from J.T.'s apartment after our little episode. I was so angry at myself that I spun like a tornado through the front door of the condo.

"You look like a Tasmanian devil on speed," said Angel, who was flipping through a magazine in the kitchen.

"Thanks," I said bitterly. I flopped on the couch, still in my coat, on the verge of tears.

"What is wrong with you?" she asked.

"I'm just the biggest idiot on the face of the planet."

"I'm sure there are some bigger than you. Don't try to take all the credit," Angel joked. But I wasn't in the mood. Angel put down the magazine then joined me on the couch. "Now tell me what's wrong."

"Where do I begin? Let's see. I was snooping through some of J.T.'s things and I ran across a picture of an old girlfriend."

"And?"

"She was kinda pretty."

"And?"

"*And*, when I asked him about her, he said he'd rather not talk about it."

"And?"

"And…I didn't like that. So I told him I had to go home."

"O….kay?"

"And he didn't even try to stop me from leaving!"

Angel looked amused. "For someone who claims she doesn't like drama, you sure are a drama queen, Shutterbug."

"No, I'm not."

"Destiny, I'm glad that grown man didn't chase after you like some lunatic. There's only room for one of those in a relationship and you've obviously volunteered for the position."

"You're not helping," I said.

"Why were you so threatened by a picture of some old girlfriend, anyway?"

"I don't know. I really don't know."

"Well, let me give you a piece of advice that you didn't ask for," Angel began. "There is nothing attractive about an insecure woman.

So you need to get it together, little sister."

My eyes were as dry as a chalk board, but I really wanted to cry. I went to my room, threw off my coat, sprawled across the bed and closed my eyes to fight the headache trying to creep into my brain. I used to get those headaches all the time after an argument with... Damian.

I cursed the day I ever let that brown-eyed bandit into my heart. It was Damian's fault I shut down and ran away from J.T. like an immature high school girl. It was his fault I felt so insecure about my ability to hold all of one man's attention without some other girl being in the back of his mind. It was his fault my heart was too battered and bruised to give it to someone who deserved it. I would never forgive Damian for sabotaging any hope of happiness in my relationship with J.T.

My headache drowned me until I fell asleep.

***

My clock read 12:07, and although it felt like I'd slept throughout the night, it was too dark to be after noon the next day. The condo was still and shadowy as I rose from my restful sleep, still wearing my clothes and shoes. I wondered if I'd missed J.T.'s call. After I turned on my lamp, I moved to my bedroom door to see if Angel had left any phone messages taped to the back of it. No messages.

I removed my clothes and left them in a pile on the floor before I stumbled into the bathroom and turned on the shower. The hot, steamy water beat my body like a drum as I closed my eyes and tried to let my mind go blank. No matter how hard I tried to wish it away, the childish behavior I displayed at J.T.'s apartment wouldn't leave my thoughts. *He must think I'm such a brat*, I thought to myself.

Freshly showered and lotioned, I put on a clean sweatshirt and a pair of comfortable flannel pants. I looked ready for bed, but I was so well-rested that sleep was the furthest thing from my mind. I sat down cross-legged on the cushiony carpet on my bedroom floor, silent, contemplating what I was going to do with myself now that the rest of the world was probably asleep. I thought about watching some T.V., but the tube had lost its appeal in the past few weeks since I'd been spending so much time with J.T.

Then I saw it. The book they say has the answer to any question. My Bible had been sitting on my nightstand ever since last Sunday. It had been a long time since I'd actually read it at home, so I placed it on my lap, and began flipping through its rugged pages. Some of the passages were underlined or highlighted; I Peter 3:3, Psalms 31, Hebrews 11:40. I searched the scriptures vigorously, desperate to find something, anything to stand out and help me make sense of this painful change I was going through. Colossians 3:12 was highlighted in blue.

As God's chosen people, holy and dearly loved, clothe yourself with compassion, kindness, humility, gentleness and patience. Bear with each other and forgive whatever grievances you may have against one another. Forgive as the Lord forgave you. And over all these virtues put on love, which binds them together in perfect unity.

"Forgive as the Lord forgave you," I said to myself. Then I closed my eyes and prayed.

***

I guess I *was* sort of a drama queen. Only a drama queen would think that it's all right to show up at a man's house uninvited at one-thirty in the morning wearing pajamas and sneakers. I knocked on J.T.'s door, hoping he wasn't asleep yet. The door crept open and J.T.'s handsome face appeared through the crack. He widened the door and I shuddered in delight at the sight of his bare chest, trying not to let it distract me as he allowed me inside.

"Have a seat," he offered cordially, but not at all in the same loving tone he usually used with me.

I sat down on the couch and he sat next to me, unusually quiet and unaffectionate, but still kind. I shifted my leg so I could face him as I began my apology.

"I know it's late, J.T., but I couldn't let another minute pass without apologizing for how I left here yesterday. I wish I could say that it wasn't like me to run away from conflict like that, but over the past two years, I guess it became quite a bad habit."

J.T. looked at me as emotionless as a soldier in formation.

I took a deep breath and continued. "I'm sorry I snooped through your things. And I'm sorry I overreacted when you didn't want to talk about your old girlfriend. I've just had bad experiences with a man I couldn't trust and who liked to argue all the time. But it wasn't fair to assume you would be the same way."

"No, it wasn't," J.T. said absolutely.

"You have been nothing but good to me ever since I met you. And you didn't deserve that."

I gently placed my hand on J.T.'s knee, hoping he would accept my peace offering.

His countenance softened.

"Baby, when I told you I was drama-free, that's exactly what I meant," he said. "I'm not into arguing, or running away or chasing after a woman instead of having normal adult conversation. I wasn't trying to hide anything from you by not talking about Shayla. I just don't see the point of rehashing details of relationships with people who are no longer in my life. Do you understand that?"

"How am I supposed to know she's no longer in your life unless you tell me?"

"I said it was old stuff, Sweetheart."

"Old stuff," I repeated. "Well I have old stuff in my life, too. And sometimes old stuff can have an effect on new stuff. So what's wrong with talking about it?"

J.T. relented. "If it's important to you, I guess it wouldn't kill me to talk about it. I'd much rather talk than have you run away from me again," he said, sounding wounded.

"I promise to talk to you about issues instead of running away from them, okay?"

"Okay. Now you go first," said J.T., with a glimmer of a smile.

I took a few moments to gather my thoughts before I told the story of the Big Bad Damian and the Evil Witch Janel. I was almost embarrassed to tell J.T. what happened. What if he thought I was weak for staying in a bad relationship? What if he thought I had bad taste in men? Or bad taste in friends?

"Damian was not very good for me," I said sadly. "We dated off and on for two years with a lot of arguing in between. Then I found out he was sleeping with one of my best friends. Now, neither one of them are in my life anymore."

The room was quiet until J.T.'s smooth voice finally shattered the silence.

"I'm sorry they hurt you," he said sincerely.

"That's old stuff, right?"

"Old stuff," he agreed.

I took a deep breath and said, "Now, it's my turn to re-open your wounds. Tell me about this Shayla girl. How long did you date her?"

"A year."

"Why'd you break up?"

J.T. gave me the most resolute, penetrating stare I'd ever seen. "Because she wasn't you."

"You can do better than that, J.T." I laughed.

"No, I can't because it's the truth."

"What do you mean, she wasn't me?" I asked, realizing his seriousness.

"I mean…she didn't have everything I wanted and needed in a woman. It just wasn't right."

"You think I'm right for you?" I asked, in hopeful amazement.

J.T. reached for my cheek with his hand and guided my lips to his. When he released his gentle kiss, he said, "I might scare you away if I answer that."

CHAPTER 18

A Private Matter

Christmas, New Year's and a few snowfalls blessed us in the next month. I managed to get a few days off from work and Angel and I celebrated the holiday in Richmond with our parents. To ring in the New Year, J.T. took me to the midnight service at church, and afterward, he gave me my Christmas present – a new lens for my camera that I had been wanting, but couldn't afford. I almost cried when I opened it.

I was much more selfish in my gift giving to J.T. His present was a rich-burgundy leather wallet with a picture of me in it. It was a lame gift, but one that he needed. One night when J.T. pulled out his wallet to pay for our dinner, I noticed that the wallet didn't look like something he would buy. It was nice enough, but something told me to ask him where he got it. He reluctantly revealed that Shayla bought it for him last year when he lost his old one. That moment, I knew exactly what I was getting J.T. for Christmas.

He just laughed when he saw the new wallet and said, "Out with old and in with the new."

That same phrase was just as appropriate for Angel's career venture. She quit her old job and opened her new public relations company in January. The first few weeks after she signed the lease, J.T., Walter and

I helped her set up office furniture and organize everything just the way she wanted. Her dream had finally come into fruition.

My life, too, was starting to shape into everything I'd envisioned it would be when I left college. I was performing well on my job, I had started looking for my own apartment, and I had someone special to help me enjoy my new city. But it was just like Damian to pop up again, just when I was feeling content. I had another voicemail message from him when I came home from work one Monday afternoon late January.

"Destiny, this is Damian again. I guess since you haven't called me back, you probably don't want to talk to me. But I figured I'd try anyway. I just wanted to let you know I'm going to be in Baltimore this week for a job interview. I decided to quit law school and try something else so…anyway. I was hoping maybe we could meet for dinner one night. Just to talk. I don't want anything but the chance to speak to you face to face. Please think about it, okay. Call me when you can. Bye."

I should've deleted the message right away. Instead, I played it again. The second time I heard it, I actually let my mind entertain the idea of meeting him for dinner. Then, the voices in my head started chattering. *Don't do it, Girl! He's a waste of time!* It wouldn't hurt to see him again. After all, you could still be friends. *Yeah, right! Friends? After what he did?* Admit you still care about him. There's nothing wrong with having dinner. *What would you tell J.T.?* J.T. doesn't have to know. *You don't need him in your life.* You know you want to see him. *No you don't!*

I deleted the message. No more drama, I told myself. I was happy and there was no need to shake things up. Unfortunately, by Thursday, I had changed my mind.

Thursday afternoon, I had a break between assignments and went home to gather my thoughts. Angel wasn't at home, so I was alone with my loud conscience and the cordless phone resting in my hand. I took a deep breath before I called Damian's cell phone. It was amazing how my fingers still knew which numbers to dial.

After about four rings, his voicemail picked up, and I left a message.

"Damian," I began, trying to sound as if it were a business call. "It's Destiny. Look. I got your message about having dinner. If you're still in town, I guess it would be all right. Call me back and tell me where to meet you. Bye."

I hung up the phone and released a hearty sigh. *What am I doing?* I asked myself. And then I answered, *I'm going on a date with the man who broke my heart.* As stupid as I felt for going through with it, I had to make sure I looked as gorgeous as I possibly could. Damian had to know that my life hadn't fallen apart without him. I had to be fabulous! So I went to my closet to select the outfit I planned to wear to my heart's funeral.

During my search for a fabulous outfit, Damian returned my phone call.

"I'm glad you called me back, Baby. I would've been disappointed if I was in your city and didn't get to see you," he said.

"What time do you want to meet?" I rushed. I already felt guilty.

"How about seven? I can pick you up if…"

"No. No, I'll meet you at the Cheesecake Factory at seven. It's on Pratt Street. Will you be able to find it?"

"Yeah. I'll make it. I can't wait to see you."

"Okay. I'll see you at seven. Bye."

I couldn't believe I was going through with it…

***

I got home just before six and quickly showered, dressed, and curled my hair. I was hoping to have all of that done before Angel came home so I wouldn't have to explain anything to her, but of all days, she came home early.

"You and J.T. got a hot date?" Angel asked, peeking into the bathroom as I applied my mascara.

"Something like that. How was your day?" I hoped she would let me change the subject.

"It was cool," she said. She went on for about five minutes about her new client while I finished putting on my make-up. Then the phone rang.

"I'll get it!" I dashed past Angel out of the bathroom and snatched up the phone in the living room. I couldn't risk having Angel answer the phone if it was Damian calling.

"Hello?" I answered, panicked. Too bad I didn't check the caller I.D. first.

"Hey, Sweetheart. How's the most beautiful woman in the world?" It was J.T.

"I'm great, Baby. How was your day?" I sounded sweet, but inside I felt as evil as the devil himself.

"It was fine. I wanted to come by tonight and see you after practice. I miss you."

"Oh, I miss you, too, Hun. But I have to work pretty late tonight. Maybe tomorrow?"

"Sure. I guess I can wait one more day." The man couldn't get any sweeter.

"Okay. I'd better get going so I'm not late."

"Okay. What time is your shoot?"

"Ummm. It should…um. Nine o'clock."

"All right. I may stop by later just to kiss you goodnight. But I'll let you go now, okay. See you soon."

"Oh. All right. Goodbye."

"Bye, Love," he said.

It was the first time I felt like I didn't deserve someone as amazing as J.T. I hated lying to him. But what man would be cool with his woman having dinner with her ex-boyfriend. Not many.

I clicked off the phone, and just as I turned around to head back to the bathroom, I ran right into Angel who must've heard my phone conversation.

"Working late? I thought you were going out with J.T.?" she inquired with suspicion.

"I didn't tell you that." I brushed her off and went to the bathroom.

She followed me.

"Destiny, I know you're not going to work dressed like that. What's up with you?"

"Nothing. Nothing's up." I frantically threw my lipstick, blush and eye liner back into my make-up bag to look busy.

"Where are you going tonight?"

"Is that any of your business?" I snapped.

"When has it not been my business? You tell me everything." Angel's hand was on her hip now.

"Not everything."

"Spill it, Destiny."

"You are making a big deal out of nothing."

"If it's not a big deal then tell me where you're going!"

"I'm going out!"

"Out with who?"

I didn't feel like explaining myself. "Please, Angel, mind your own business just this once. I don't ask very often. This is a private matter, okay?"

"A private matter?"

"Yes! Private!"

"You must have forgotten who you're talking to. I know every embarrassing, heartbreaking, agonizing moment of your life. You've never kept private matters from me before."

"All you're going to do is tell me what a big mistake I'm making and how stupid I am for going."

"Then it must be a stupid thing to do! I've never given you bad advice. Have I?"

"Whatever, Angel. This time I don't want your advice."

"Do whatever you want! I don't care!" she yelled.

Angel stormed out of the bathroom and up the stairs to her room. How dare she say she didn't care about me! What kind of sister was she?

"Oh, so now you're mad at me!" I followed her as far as the steps and yelled at her from the bottom of the stairs. "You want to know so bad? I'll tell you. I'm going to dinner with Damian, okay? Now you know all my business!"

I darted into my room, probably angrier at myself than Angel. I sat on my bed in a huff and waited for Angel's inevitable presence.

She finally came downstairs and appeared in the doorway of my bedroom.

"Either I'm crazy or you just told me you're having dinner with the same man who cheated on you with your best friend. Please tell me I'm crazy."

I sat in silence, legs crossed, and pretended to be all-consumed by my need for a manicure.

"Shutter, have you lost your mind? How could you go on a date with him after what he put you through?"

"See, I knew you would have something to say!"

"Why wouldn't I have something to say? *Someone* needs to talk you out of this foolishness. Why are you going out with him?"

"It's just something I need to do, okay? I need closure so I can move on with my life."

"I thought you were already moving on! You have a wonderful man who cares about you. And speaking of that wonderful man, what does J.T. think about all this?"

As if I needed to feel any more guilty…

"J.T. doesn't need to know. It's just dinner. It's not like I'm cheating on him. Just please, don't say anything to him. He wouldn't understand."

"You didn't give him a chance to. I can't believe you lied to him, Destiny. That's not like you."

"He wouldn't understand!"

"You keep telling yourself that!" Angel looked disgusted with me. "Look...you're going to do what you want to do anyway. So I'm done talking. But I *will* say this. You will regret lying to your boyfriend, and you will probably regret this little secret affair you're having with Damian. Have a great time!" she said with contempt.

Angel disappeared from sight, leaving me alone feeling like a Jezebel. She was making such a huge deal out of nothing! I glanced over at my clock that read six-forty. I tossed the pros and cons of going on this date around in my head for the next ten minutes. Even though I found no pros, I picked up my purse, put on my coat, and went out on a date with the man I thought I would never forgive.

CHAPTER 19

Damian Frost

I was beginning to think Destiny wasn't going to call me while I was in Baltimore. But even if she didn't, I still planned to see her before I left. I knew that even after all we'd been through, she still had love for me and there was a chance, although slim, that she would eventually take me back.

As I drove to the restaurant where I was supposed to meet her for dinner, I reminisced about the first time I laid eyes on Destiny. She had this smile that demanded to be returned. Her disposition was so happy and friendly. She was almost too sweet for me to date. But the more I got to know her, the more I grew to love her innocence. I also grew to love the way she fit into her jeans. That's really where our problems began.

My Destiny was one of those religious types. She wanted to wait until she was married before she had sex, but I couldn't wait for that. I was a grown man and I wanted to do what grown men do. She eventually gave in and we had a great sex life until she started feeling guilty. She finally cut me off from sex because she didn't want to "offend her spirit" anymore - whatever that means. She was still my woman, but I had to find a way to handle my business, if you know what I mean.

I never meant for her to find out about my indiscretion with her friend, Janel. Then again, no man wants to get caught cheating. Out of all the stupid things I've done in my life, I wish I could take that one back. It was just sex. Simple as that. But women never see it that way.

Ever since Destiny and I broke up I tried to convince myself that I didn't love her anymore and that I was free to do anything I wanted. But I knew I would never find another woman like her. She was a good girl. Beautiful inside and out. I just wasn't ready to be tied down to one woman yet. I was only 24-years-old! I had lots of things to see and do before I settled down with anyone. But I knew in my heart that Destiny was who I eventually wanted. I truly believed that's what she was...my Destiny.

My mom loved her, too. My dad always asked me when I was going to marry her. But their approval of our relationship only made me question it more. My dad was forever trying to push me into doing things I didn't want to do. Exhibit A: law school. I didn't really know what the hell I wanted to do. I just knew I wasn't ready for marriage. But if that's what it would take to get Destiny back, I was prepared to do it.

I pulled into a parking space at the Cheesecake Factory and checked my breath before I went inside. It wasn't likely that I'd get a hello-kiss, but a brother could dream, right? I searched the restaurant lobby for any sign of Destiny, but there was none. So, I gave my name to the hostess to put on the waiting list and sat down on a bench to watch the door.

Seven-ten. Seven-fifteen. Seven-twenty. I was beginning to wonder if she'd changed her mind about meeting me. She really had no reason to have dinner with me unless there was a chance of us getting back together. I was hopeful that was the case. Destiny's angelic face finally appeared in the small crowd that had gathered in the lobby. Her hair was pinned up in loose black curls and she had a red scarf around her neck. I stood to my feet and waited for her to catch sight of me.

"Destiny!" I called to speed up the process. She shifted her eyes around the room until she saw mine. I held my breath and waited for that smile that kept appearing in my dreams at night. What she gave me was far less than I'd hoped for.

"Hi, Damian," she said as she approached me. No smile in sight.

"Hey, Baby Girl." I disregarded her standoffishness and grabbed her into my arms like she was still mine. "I missed you."

She reluctantly hugged me back.

"Here. Let me take your coat," I offered.

She unbuttoned her coat and slipped out of it as I assisted her like a gentleman.

"Come have a seat. Our table should be ready in a few minutes."

Destiny sat down on the bench just as the buzzer in my hand began to light up and vibrate.

"That's us," I said.

We checked in at the front desk then followed the host to our table. We arranged ourselves and our coats into the chairs as the host handed us our menus.

"You look beautiful tonight," I said peeking at Destiny over my menu.

"Thank you," she replied. Her eyes never shifted from whatever meal description she was considering. We placed our drink and dinner orders without much conversation. Then finally, we had nothing to do but talk to each other.

"You look really...really beautiful tonight," I repeated. It was one way to break the ice.

"You said that already." She finally gave me a glimmer of a smile.

"It deserved repeating."

"You were always so charming, Damian," she said, her tone exaggerated. She was finally starting to warm up to me again.

"You used to love that about me."

"Anyway," she brushed me off. "How did your interview go today? I was surprised to hear you quit law school."

"Yeah. I was tired of law school and working with my dad, so I've been interviewing for a bunch of different jobs. I'm really interested in pharmaceutical sales, though. I've applied for a job here, in Atlanta and Dallas."

"Good for you," she said with genuine pride. "I'm glad you finally decided to do what you want instead of what your dad thinks is best. I'm sure it was a tough decision for you to quit school."

"It was. But I think it'll be good to move away and do my own thing from now on." I took a sip of my water.

"I think you would be perfect for sales, as much as you like to sweet-talk people," she said, loosening up even more.

"We'll see. I don't have the job yet. So, how's life been treating you lately? How's work?"

"Work is great. I'm getting some interesting photo assignments and I'm taking on freelance jobs here and there."

"Good."

I paused for a moment to admire the way her eyes reflected the dim lights. She wore a black sweater pulled down below her smooth, brown shoulders. I just wanted to reach over and feel her soft skin again.

"It's so crazy that you're here with me right now," I said. "I thought I would never have the chance to talk to you face to face. There was so much I wanted to say to you that night, but…"

I saw her take a deep breath as if she were bracing herself for the topic. Maybe it was too soon in the evening to bring up the unpleasant past.

"Damian, please. We don't need to go there, okay? I didn't come here to talk about that."

"I hope you don't mind me asking, Baby, but why did you come here?" I asked inquisitively. "I'm glad you did, but I must admit I was a little surprised."

"I guess I just wanted to know that you're okay, you know? Two years is a long time to spend with someone and then just call it quits. We used to be good friends and I want you to know that even with all the ups and downs of our relationship, I don't regret one single moment. What we had together led me to where I am today. And I'm happy. I want you to be happy, too."

I looked at her thoughtfully. That moment, I knew I had some competition. She had to have another man in her life or she wouldn't be feeding me all this 'happiness' crap.

"I'm glad that you're happy, Destiny. But it was all I could do not to kiss you when I saw you come through that door."

"Damian, I…"

"I'm gonna be kicking myself for the rest of my life knowing I messed things up between us. But I'm really glad you came here tonight. I didn't want to live the rest of my life knowing that you hate me."

"No, I don't hate you," she said tenderly.

"Your new man is lucky," I said, glancing up to check out her reaction.

"I didn't tell you I had a new man." She smiled as if I had figured out her little secret that she secretly wanted me to know.

"I can see it in your eyes."

"Well, I'm sure you don't spend too many nights alone either, Damian."

"No, not too many; but I'll never find another Destiny."

"You will find your destiny some day," she assured.

Little did she know that I had already found my destiny. I just screwed things up with her.

The waiter interrupted our conversation and placed our meals in front of us. Destiny reached out her open hand to me just as I was about to heap a forkful of food into my mouth.

"Oh, sorry," I said. I took her hand and she said grace before we ate.

"So how long have you been seeing this guy?" I asked. I was a little disgruntled by the fact that she was already seeing someone else. It was going to be hard enough getting her back without some other man being in the way.

"Not long. About three months," she answered between bites.

"It sure didn't take you long to get over me, did it?"

She shot me an evil look that would scare the stripes off a zebra.

"Don't even go there, Damian," she warned. We ate in silence for a few minutes while I tried to think of a way to recover from my fumble.

"You know what I was thinking about on the drive up here?" I asked.

"What?"

"You remember that vacation we took in Florida that summer? With Mike and his girl?"

"Yeah, I remember."

"We had a lot of fun, huh?" I asked. She nodded.

"You remember when we spent the whole day on the beach…riding on jet skis and paddle boats…laying out in the sun until it went down that night? That was the most fun I've ever had in my life."

"Yeah. It was fun," she said, almost reminiscing with me.

"We had a lot of good times together, Destiny. I know we had some bad ones, but we had a lot of good ones, too."

"I know," she said, sounding a little sad.

"Sometimes I wish we could just go back to those times. I miss seeing your smile and hearing you laugh. I miss seeing you that happy."

Destiny sighed and stirred her tea with a straw.

"Things change, Damian. I guess at some point it wasn't enough to see me happy. If things were so good, why did you feel the need to be with someone else? My best friend at that?"

I released a breath and tried to concoct an explanation that wouldn't leave me looking like the bad guy. But I guess I already was the bad guy. So the only thing I could come up with was the truth.

"Baby, I know this sounds cold, but it was just sex. When you and I stopped sleeping together, I was with Janel for sex and nothing else. I'm just being honest."

A pained look appeared on her face as she digested the news she had probably been wondering about since she found out about me and Janel. I wished there was a way I could make it up to her.

"I'm so sorry I hurt you, Destiny. I wish I could take it all back. You were the best thing that ever happened to me and I…I let you down. I'm sorry."

Destiny took her napkin off her lap and placed it on the table. "Excuse me for a minute," she said, standing up. She picked up her purse, too.

"No, wait. Baby, please don't leave."

"I don't even know what I'm doing here," she said.

"Please stay with me. Don't go just yet."

I stood up and gently held her arm to sway her decision to stay. A few table neighbors began to stare, but I didn't care. I couldn't let her leave.

"Just let me go to the bathroom, okay," she insisted. "I'll be back."

She took off in the direction of the bathroom, which eased my mind. But I watched the door to make sure she didn't try to sneak out. I felt like I was blowing my chance to make things right with her.

A few minutes later Destiny returned to the table as promised. She sat down but seemed to have abandoned the idea of finishing her dinner.

"Are you done eating?" I asked.

"Yes, I'm full. I'll take it home and eat it for lunch tomorrow."

I pushed my plate to the side and gazed across the table at the love of my life. She couldn't even look me in the eye.

"I should go, Damian. We've talked, we had dinner. I have to go to work early tomorrow."

"Okay. Just let me take care of this and I'll walk you to your car."

I beckoned the waiter to bring our check, gave him my credit card, and waited for him to bring the receipt.

There was awkward silence between us as we waited for the waiter until Destiny asked,

"Why did you want to see me tonight?"

"Truth be told, I still love you, Baby. There's probably not even a slim chance that you would consider starting a brand new relationship with me. But I figured if you cared enough to meet me for dinner... maybe, somewhere deep down inside, you still have love for me. You have to know I'm a different man. I would never do anything to hurt you again. You have to believe me."

"Damian, I can't go back to you."

"Shhh. Just...don't say anything, okay. I'll be patient. I'll wait for you to decide what you want."

"You don't understand. I've moved on. I'm in love...with someone else. Someone who behaves like a king and makes me feel like a queen. As a matter of fact, I don't even know why I'm here with you when I could be spending time with him."

Her words burned me a little bit, but only the strongest survive. He couldn't be that special if she agreed to go on a date with me.

"I can respect that, Baby. I can respect that. Just let me walk you to your car before you go."

The waiter finally brought the receipt for me to sign. I left the tip and popped a free mint into my mouth. Destiny stood up and put on her coat before I could get to her. She was obviously in a hurry to leave. I followed her out of the restaurant and thanked the waiter as we passed him on the way out the door. Destiny walked quickly through the parking lot to her car, clinching her coat closed to fight off the wind.

"Slow down," I called to her.

"It's cold out here," was her reply. When she got to her car, she paused long enough to say, "Thanks for dinner. It was nice seeing you again."

I opened her car door, but before I let her in, I pulled her close to me.

"Thank *you* for dinner," I said, ready to make my final attempt at winning her heart back. I tried to kiss her, but she violently pushed me away and gave me a razor-sharp glare.

"There are no more butterflies, Damian. It's over. Don't call me anymore."

She got in her car and drove away, leaving me looking like a fool in the cold. Getting her back was going to be harder than I thought.

As I walked back through the parking lot, I noticed our waiter was trying to flag me down.

"Sir! You left these at your table!" he called. I went to him and retrieved two carry out boxes of food and Destiny's red scarf.

CHAPTER 20

Walking On Eggshells

I must've been crazy to think anything good would come of going out with Damian. He was still the same charming, arrogant, selfish, stubborn man he always was. I felt like a fool for even wasting my time with him – even if I got a free meal out of the evening.

I was so thankful that the overwhelming experience was over. It was about nine-thirty when I came into the quiet condo and crept into my room to disrobe. But I had barely made it out of my slacks when the phone rang.

"Hello?" I answered.

"Hey, Sweetheart. I'm outside," said J.T. "I just wanted to call before I came in so I wouldn't show up unannounced."

"All right, Baby. Come on in," I said as I tore off my pants and my sweater and threw on my pajamas in a mad dash.

I did my best to tone down my make up and rumple my hair before I went to let J.T. inside.

"Hey, Baby!" I exclaimed as I hugged J.T.'s neck.

"Mmmmm," he moaned as he squeezed me back. "You smell good." He kissed my neck.

"You must've finished work early."

"Yeah, a little," I said as he came inside. "I'm glad you came by."

"I had to see you. I've missed these lips." J.T. leaned into me and enveloped my lips into his like he hadn't seen me in ages. He backed me up onto the couch and ending up lacing me with hundreds of soft, moist kisses I felt I didn't deserve. They felt so good, though. But I felt guilty about lying to him. I tried to push him off of me so I could confess, but his lips felt too, too good.

"J.T., I have to tell you something," I said between breathless kisses.

"What is it, Sweetheart?" he asked, but didn't stop kissing me.

Then there was a bang on the door.

We both froze and so did my heart when I realized who it could've been. J.T. raised himself off of me and offered to answer it.

"No, Baby. I'll get it," I insisted.

With each step I took, the sound of my heart thumped louder and louder in my ears. And wouldn't you know it? The peephole was covered up. It couldn't be anyone other than Damian.

I didn't know whether to open it or pretend no one was home. But I didn't want to alarm J.T. He was already leery of someone being at our door this late. I took a deep breath and opened the door.

"Hey," said Damian, holding my scarf and a Styrofoam carry-out box. "You forgot your food at the restaurant. And you left your scarf, too. I was going to keep it because it smelled like your perfume. But I didn't want your pretty neck to get cold."

"Thanks," I said, snatching my scarf. "You can keep the food. Have a good night." I began to close the door, but Damian stopped it.

"Wait. You said you wanted to eat it for lunch tomorrow. You don't want this good food to go to waste, do you?"

"Okay, I'll take it," I rushed, praying he would just go away.

"Aren't you going to invite me in?"

"No, now will you please leave? I told you not to call me anymore. That means no house calls," I snapped, trying not to let J.T. hear. But it was too late.

"What's wrong, Sweetheart?" J.T.'s baritone voice projected out into the night air as he widened the door and examined our unwanted guest. "Who's this?"

Damian looked as if he'd seen his worst enemy. "I'm Damian. And you must be the king," he said, with a sarcastic smile.

"I think it's time for you to go, Damian," I interjected. I didn't like where this scene was heading.

"Destiny told me all about you at dinner tonight," Damian continued. "She left her scarf and her leftovers so I thought I'd drop them by. Nice to meet you..." Damian stuck out his hand for J.T. to shake.

"J.T." J.T said, defensively, declining his offer. "Dinner, huh? Well that was nice of you to drop them by. Now if you'll excuse us."

"Oh, you didn't know about our little dinner date?" Damian asked. "We had a good time. We reminisced about all the things we used to do together. But you know what? I'm glad to see she's found someone who..." Damian dramatically looked J.T. up and down. "Someone who probably reminds her of me. Tall, dark, handsome, athletic. Your taste sure hasn't changed, Baby," he said, now looking at me.

"Okay, goodbye, Damian," I rushed. I tried to push J.T.'s strong body back inside the condo without success.

"I think it's time for you to go, Man," J.T. said, standing in front of me and entering into Damian's space. In a stern, powerful voice, he continued, "I don't appreciate you coming to my lady's house and disrespecting her wishes when she's asked you to leave."

"All, right. All right, bruh. Step back. I'm not trying to start nothing," Damian said, backing away from the door. "Thanks for taking such good care of my woman for me. I'll be back for her."

J.T. and I watched Damian pull off in his car and disappear from sight before we went back inside the condo. I went inside slowly and timidly like I was walking on eggshells. I knew it wasn't going to be a good night. I busied myself by putting the food in the refrigerator and hanging up my scarf so the evidence of my crime was out of sight.

J.T. sat on the couch in silence, patiently waiting for me to say something. I was hesitant to go near him or look him in the eye. It scared me to think that he may never look at me the same way he used to.

"Why don't you come sit down and talk to me," he said, finally getting annoyed by my procrastination. I went to the couch and sat next to him, still unable to look him in the eye.

"I have...an apology to make," I began. I realized that this was the second time I had to come to J.T. for forgiveness for my behavior. I wasn't used to being the one in a relationship who had to apologize all the time, and I sure didn't like it.

"I wasn't honest with you when I said I had to work late tonight."

J.T.'s jaw muscle began to tighten and his eyes were in a hard stare at the floor.

"You were with him, I take it?" he asked in a cold tone.

"Yes. I'm sorry I lied to you. I just didn't think you'd understand why I wanted to see him again."

"Why did you want to see him?" he snapped, and fired his eyes at me. "Isn't this the same guy who messed around with your friend?"

"Yes," I admitted, with my head bowed like a puppy.

J.T. smirked and shook his head. "Then why? Why couldn't you just tell me instead of lying? I'm not saying I wouldn't have been happy about you seeing this guy, but I would've trusted you to do right by me. But now I don't know. You really shouldn't have lied to me, Destiny. I don't do well with liars."

"J.T., I can't begin to tell you how sorry I am. It's not like me to say things that aren't true, but...I just didn't know how to explain this to you."

"Well I need you to try," he said, slightly raising his voice. "Because this is not cool with me. I can handle a lot of things in a relationship, but lying is not one of them. I thought we were better than that. I thought you knew you could talk to me about anything."

I begged myself not to cry. I felt like I was being chastised by my father. I swallowed the lump in my throat and tried to decide if I should talk my way out of this or keep my mouth shut.

"It was nothing. Nothing is going on between me and Damian! I promise you!" I whined, so angry at myself for letting this get out of hand. I couldn't bare the thought of losing J.T.

"Then why did you lie to me about going to see him?"

"Because I wanted to make sure there was nothing left between us," I admitted. "I wanted to make sure my heart was free and clear to love again. And it is. I only want you in my life."

"You should've made sure your heart was free and clear before I gave you mine!" he said, angrily.

He was right. Maybe I rushed into my relationship with J.T. But I didn't regret it.

J.T. looked disappointed and hurt. I reached out my hand to touch his face, but he pulled away from me - for the first time ever. I sat back into the couch and crossed my arms. All I could do was to say that I was sorry. The rest was up to him - even though I prayed it wouldn't take him long to forgive me. We sat in silence for what seemed like decades.

All the emotion from the evening was beginning to drain me.

"What can I say to make things right again?" I asked in a soft voice. "It was a big mistake. I can't fix what happened, but I can promise you it won't ever happen again. You can trust me, J.T."

"No. I thought I could trust you. But tonight proved that I can't."

"Please forgive me, Baby," I pleaded. "I just want to be your Sweetheart again."

J.T. remained speechless for a few moments.

"I'm gonna leave now," he said. "It doesn't mean I'm running away from our conflict. I just need to clear my head tonight, all right?"

A stream of tears ran down my face. J.T. stood up from the couch and I followed him to the door, hoping he would stay long enough to forgive me. Before he opened the door, he lifted his hand to wipe a few tears from my eyes. Then he left me standing alone in the living room.

That weekend was the first weekend I'd spent away from J.T since we first met – and I thought it would kill me. If he was trying to teach me a lesson, it was working because all I could do was think about how stupid I was for jeopardizing such a perfect relationship for one that was so flawed.

We spoke on the phone everyday, although the conversations never lasted more than five minutes. J.T. said he needed time to sort some things out. I didn't care how many times I had to apologize or how long it would take him to get over it. I wanted my man back.

CHAPTER 21

Another Blast From My Past

After being deprived of J.T.'s affection all weekend, I thought Monday couldn't be any worse. I was wrong. I ran over a nail with my car, which flattened my tire, which made me late for my photo assignment, which made me miss the shot I needed for the paper. To top it all off, I got a speeding ticket on the way home for driving 53 in a 45 mile per hour zone…as if I needed another bill that month. Just when I thought the day couldn't possibly get worse, another blast from my past hit me like a drunk-driver.

It was six-thirty that evening and I had just gotten home from working out at the gym to relieve my stressful day.

"We need to get you a cell phone," Angel said, as I came through the front door of the condo. She was sitting on the couch flipping through files and papers. "Vanessa's called here three times looking for you."

"Did she say what was wrong?" I asked.

"No, but it sounded pretty urgent. You should call her now."

I dropped my gym bag on the floor and went to pick up the cordless phone on the arm of the couch. Just as I was about to dial Vanessa's number, the phone rang in my hand.

"Hello?" I answered.

"Is this Destiny?"

"Yes. Who is this?"

"This is Gina, Honey. I know it's been a long time since we've spoken, but I need you to come to Durham right away."

"Oh, Ms. Washington…I didn't recognize your voice," I said, stunned when I finally discerned the voice of Janel's mother on the other end of the phone. "What's the matter?"

"I thought you and Vanessa would have been here by now, but I guess you hadn't heard," she said, sounding as if she had been crying. "Janel…she's been in a terrible car accident. She lost the baby and the doctors don't know if Janel will make it either."

Baby? Oh, my God!

"What happened?" I asked in astonishment. "I didn't even know… When did this happen?"

"This morning," she replied. "I don't know all the details of the accident, but Janel is at Duke Medical Center in critical condition. Please come if you can, Destiny. I've already called Vanessa and she said she'd come after she got off from work."

"Ms. Washington, I…Janel and I… we…" I couldn't put the right words together. How could I tell her mother that Janel and I were no longer friends because she slept with my ex-boyfriend? It sounded so juvenile and irrelevant at the moment.

Ms. Washington continued. "Honey, I think the doctor is coming with more news, so I'm going to let you go. Please just come, okay. I'm sure Janel would want her friends here with her. Oh, Lord, please let her be all right," she begged.

"I'll try to come," I said, with shrouded hesitation.

"Okay, I've got to go now. I'll see you when you get here."

I hung up the phone slowly and raised my eyes to meet Angel's anxious stare.

"What happened?" she asked.

"Janel was in a car accident," I said in disbelief. "She's in critical condition and her mother wants me to go down there to see her."

"Whaaaaat? What are you going to do?"

"That isn't even the worst of it, Angel." I took a few steps and plopped down on the couch next to her. "She was pregnant...and she lost the baby."

Angel gasped. "Oh, my God!"

"I can't believe she was going to have a baby and I didn't even know."

My heart went out to Janel and I truly hoped that she would be all right. But suddenly my gut tightened when it crossed my mind that Damian could've been the father.

"What if it was Damian's baby?" I asked, awestruck.

"I don't know, Shutter," Angel said, shaking her head. "I'm not sure if I can help you with this one. You've got to decide whether you can push that issue aside long enough to make amends with Janel. You may not get another chance."

I wasn't sure if I could swallow my pride and stand by Janel's side yet again. It was as if an angel and a devil were on each shoulder coaxing me to do what they wanted. The little devil said I had no business worrying about someone who betrayed me the way Janel did. My angel told me to pack my bag, drive to Durham and see Janel, because it might be the last time I'd ever lay eyes on her.

Call me stupid. Call me predictable. But my angel won. I showered, packed, and had my Altima on I-95 South within an hour. Angel objected to me leaving so late, but I wouldn't have been able to sleep without knowing what was going on with Janel.

The five-hour drive wasn't nearly enough time to comprehend just exactly what I was doing or why I was doing it. The whole gamut of emotions rushed through my body. I was afraid for Janel's life. I felt sadness at the loss of her baby. A part of me felt guilty for not being there for someone I used to call my best friend. I couldn't even imagine what Janel had been going through these past few months without me and Vanessa. But a larger part of me was angry that Janel was still able to drag me back into her mess.

What was I doing? Why was I going back there?

***

The hospital was eerily quiet. It was just after midnight when I arrived, and the receptionist gave me a hard time about seeing Janel after visiting hours. After driving all the way from Maryland, I had no intention of taking 'no' for an answer. Luckily, Janel's mother came down the hall during our confrontation and told the receptionist that I was family and Janel wanted to see me.

Ms. Washington hugged me tight when she saw me. I hadn't seen her in quite a long time. Although she looked weary, she was just as attractive as always - an older version of Janel.

"Thank you so much for coming, Honey," said Ms. Washington as she released our hug. "Janel is in stable condition now. I know she'll be happy to see you." She held my hand and guided me to Janel's room.

Just before Ms. Washington opened the door to Janel's room, I froze. I had no idea what I was going to say to her, or if I wanted to hear anything she had to say. I just needed to know if she was all right.

I followed Ms. Washington into the dimly lit room, and then I saw Janel lying in that hospital bed – scarred, pale, tired, but beautiful nonetheless. I couldn't believe my friend almost lost her life. Well, I guess she was my ex-friend now. Either way, my heart saddened at the sight of her.

"Janel, Honey. Look who's here to see you," said Ms. Washington, standing at Janel's bedside and clutching her hand.

Janel's eyes widened as she saw me.

"Destiny…" she said, in utter disbelief. She stretched out her slim hand for me to take, but I hesitated to go to her. I glanced over at Ms. Washington's pained faced. She had no idea what had happened between me and Janel.

I reluctantly inched toward my ex-friend and took her hand, which sent a look of relief across Janel's face. All I could feel was numbness.

"I'll leave you two alone," said Ms. Washington, heading toward the door. "I'm going to get some coffee. I'll be right back."

Ms. Washington left the room and closed the door behind her. I felt awkward holding Janel's hand, so I let it go, not really sure what to do next.

"I don't even know what to say," I said softly.

"You don't have to say anything. I'm just glad you came."

Janel sounded exhausted. "Please sit."

She patted a space on her bed for me to sit down, but I declined. I was determined not get too comfortable around her.

"So, how do you feel?" I asked.

"I don't feel much of anything right now. But it hurts to move. I'm still pretty sore."

"What happened?"

She spoke slowly as she described the incident.

"I was driving on a two-lane highway. Someone tried to pass the car that was coming toward me and I swerved to miss it. I ran off the side of the road, hit the railing and ran into some trees. I don't remember much else. What a way to start the day, huh?" she said, slightly smiling. I guess she was attempting to add humor to the conversation.

My face grew somber.

"I'm sorry to hear about the baby," I said.

"Who told you?" Janel asked, as if she had been betrayed.

I hesitated to respond. Maybe I shouldn't have brought it up.

"Your mom mentioned it when she called," I said, as innocently as I could.

Janel smirked. "I guess God didn't think I'd make a very good mother."

"Don't say that."

"Why not? It's the truth. What kind of a mother would I be?"

Janel quickly shifted into her woe-is-me mode that I knew so well. But if there was ever a time I needed to encourage her, it was now.

"You can be any kind of mother you want to be, Janel. I don't understand why you could never see what everybody else sees in you. Or more importantly what God sees in you."

"What does He see? Tell me that, Destiny, since you claim to know Him so well," she said, raising her voice. "Tell me what God sees in a girl who sleeps around with all kinds of men; a girl who betrayed her best friend; a girl who already…murdered two of her babies…" She covered her mouth and groaned from the pain of her tears.

"Please don't cry," I said, hoping Janel's mother wouldn't come into the room and wonder what I did to make her daughter bawl.

I moved over to her bed and sat down next to her.

"Listen to me, Janel. Let me tell you what *I* see in you. I see someone who has spent her whole life chasing love that she already has. You are wise enough to know that nothing you have done is too great for God's forgiveness."

"I feel like He's punishing me for all the wrong I've done," Janel cried. "I don't know how to fix this. I'm so tired of hurting myself and everyone around me. I don't want to be this person anymore."

"You don't have to be. You need to change the way you see yourself. Ask Him to help you change the way you live. Life can be so good when you live it the right way."

Janel closed her eyes as more tears gushed down her face. I'd never seen someone so sad.

"I'm so sorry I hurt you, Destiny," she whimpered as softly as a little child.

I felt so sorry for her. I stayed with her and held her hand until her sobs faded. Her chest began to rise and fall slowly, and she eventually drifted into sleep. She looked so peaceful, so beautiful. I gently rested my hand on her head and prayed a silent prayer for her. And then I asked God to forgive me for hating her so much.

CHAPTER 22

Guardian Angel

It was almost two o'clock in the morning when I left the hospital. Mrs. Washington, who had driven over two hours from Charlotte, offered to let me stay in her hotel room, but I ended up spending the night at Vanessa's new apartment. I needed to get away from all the madness I had just experienced.

When I woke up in an unfamiliar bed, I had almost forgotten where I was. Vanessa had already left for work and she told me she would meet me for lunch at noon. I glanced over at the clock on her night stand that read 8:35 a.m. "Crap!" I exclaimed, remembering I had a job to go to. I stumbled around Vanessa's bedroom looking for a phone so I could call John and tell him I had to leave town for a family emergency and I would be back tomorrow. He was understanding and didn't give me a hard time because it was the first time I'd ever asked for a day off.

Then I called Angel at work to let her know I had made it to North Carolina and that Janel was doing fine.

I hung up the phone, prepared to make one more call. But I knew J.T. wouldn't be able to answer his phone until his next break from class. I called his cell phone number and left a message anyway.

"J.T. It's me. I just wanted to let you know that I had to make an emergency trip to North Carolina, but I made it all right. I'm at Vanessa's apartment. Please call me here when you get a chance. (919) 555-6709. I....I miss you."

The words 'I love you' were dangerously close to escaping from my lips. I realized that I loved J.T. a long time ago, but I was afraid of making that same mistake twice. The last person I loved didn't love me back the way I needed him to. So, I decided to leave that word out of my vocabulary for now. At least until I was sure he felt the same about me.

I hung up the phone and tried to go back to sleep. But it was glaringly sunny that morning. The light of day flooded the room, making it impossible for me to forget where I was. I gave up on the possibility of sleep and headed to the bathroom to bathe.

I made myself at home in Vanessa's new apartment that had only been standing for a month. She already had it fashionably decorated in crimson and cream, accentuated with elephants and other paraphernalia representing her sorority. I managed to find a bowl and a box of Frosted Flakes in her kitchen then I watched a little T.V. while I ate breakfast.

Around 10:30 a.m., Vanessa's phone rang. I recognized J.T.'s cell phone number on the caller I.D. screen.

"Hello?" I answered.

"It's me, Sweetheart. Are you all right?"

"Yeah, I'm okay," I said, glad I was still his Sweetheart.

"Angel told me about what happened to your friend."

"Friend. Yeah."

"Did you get a chance to see her?"

"Yeah, I did. She's doing fine."

"I would've taken you down there. You didn't have to go alone." The concern in his voice made me love him another inch more.

"That's sweet of you, but I'm okay. I needed the time to think anyway," I lied. It would've been nice to have him to talk to.

"Well, I wish you had a cell phone so you could call me on the road in case you needed me. I was worried to death about you."

"I'm sorry. I guess I need to break down and join the rest of the cellular world," I joked, trying to cover up the increased pitch of my voice. I was slowly being overcome by all the recent disruptions in my life. First, Damian - now Janel. Why couldn't they both just stay out of my life?

"Are you crying?"

"A little," I sniffed. "But I'm okay. I just don't know what to do or how to feel. This whole thing is just so complicated."

"What do you mean?"

Annoying tears filled my eyes. I thought I had cried my last cry over Janel, but I guess I had never really dealt with my feelings about not having her as my friend anymore.

"Have you ever hated someone you love?" I asked. "Or loved someone you hated?"

"Hate is a pretty strong word. I don't think I've ever hated anyone."

"I think I hate her, J.T. I've never hated anyone before, but I hate Janel. And now I'm down here for her and I don't know why."

"Is she the girl who...you know... with your ex-boyfriend?"

"Yeah. Isn't this crazy?"

"Not for someone like you. I don't think you hate her, Destiny. You just hate what she did."

"I don't even know why she wanted me to come down here."

"Maybe she wanted to apologize."

"J.T., she's got bigger problems in life than what she did to me. She just lost her baby for God's sake!"

I held my head in my free hand and cried into the phone while J.T. waited patiently for me to get myself together. I was so tired of crying.

"Our friendship could never survive what she did to me," I continued. "But I still care about her. I still want things to work out for her. We were friends for a long time, you know?"

"I know, Baby. I wish I could be there with you right now. I know this is hard for you."

"I'll be all right. I'm going to check on her later today and I'll probably drive back after that."

"All right. Hey, before you go, close your eyes for a second so I can pray for you."

I couldn't believe my ears, but I did as I was told. J.T. cleared his throat.

"All right. Um, Lord, we come to You as humbly as we know how. We thank You for allowing us to see this day and for blessing us with such a wonderful relationship. God, right now Your daughter Destiny is hurting and confused, but we both know that although we may not understand Your plan, it is perfect. So, we lift the situation up to You and ask that You give us peace while You're working it out. We say a special prayer for Destiny's friend in the hospital. Speak to her and give her Your divine guidance. We ask these things in the name of Your son, Jesus. Amen."

My eyes leaked like a faucet.

"That was beautiful, J.T. Thank you."

"You come home to me safely, Sweetheart. Call me if you need anything. To talk or whatever."

"I will."

***

"It feels weird eating here without Janel," said Vanessa, as she sipped her lemonade. We were dining at our favorite hang-out place when we were in college – a family-owned soul food joint that was responsible for many cases of the freshman fifteen. Nostalgia rushed over me as we ate at the same table where we always used to sit - minus one.

"It hasn't even been a year since we graduated and so much has changed," I said. "This isn't how I pictured our reunion."

"How did she look last night?" Vanessa asked.

"She's stable, but she looks pretty beat up. Her mother seemed so sad."

"I can imagine. She lost her grandchild and almost lost her daughter. What about you? Are you all right?" she asked, with concern in her eyes.

"Not really. I just wish I knew why all this mess is happening. I don't even know why I came all the way down here for her. I shouldn't even care anymore, but I do."

"I know why you're here. You're that girl's guardian angel, Destiny. You have been ever since you met her."

"Guardian angel? Whatever. I'm the girl whose boyfriend she slept with."

"No, you're the person who loves her in spite of that," Vanessa continued. "I never understood why you continued to be her friend after all the crap she's pulled in the past four years. And this tops it all. But where are you? Right by her side. A guardian angel."

"I must not be a very good guardian. I didn't even know she was pregnant."

"Neither did I. And I was living with her."

"You know, I can't help but think that Damian could've been the baby's father," I said solemnly. "I wonder if he even knows what happened."

"I don't know, Girl. There's really nothing we can do about any of this except to pray for Janel."

"Yeah, you're right."

We continued our lunch in silence for awhile. When I looked up from my plate, I noticed Vanessa's mind was somewhere else.

"Is everything, okay?" I asked. "With all this talk about Janel, I didn't get a chance to see how you're doing?"

"I'm doing fine, Girl. My mom is just getting on my nerves with all this wedding planning. I just want to get it over with so Rodney and I can get to honeymooning!"

"I know that's right!" I exclaimed, and gave Vanessa a girlfriend high-five. "Are you gonna let me do the photography for the wedding? You can't let just anyone handle pictures for your special day."

"No! I need you to stand next to me as my maid of honor."

"Oh, yeah. I haven't been officially invited to be your maid of honor, so I didn't know..." I said teasingly.

"Oh, please! You know you're my girl! You'd better be right there beside me to make sure I don't fall on my face."

"You know I'll be there for you, Nessa."

I fed the last scoop of mashed potatoes to my mouth as I thought for a moment.

"Do you plan to invite Janel?" I asked.

"I don't know. I always imagined both of you being my bridesmaids. But I don't want things to be awkward for you."

"No, Girl, it's your day. I'll be cool with whatever you decide."

"We're really not as close as we used to be ever since I moved out. I don't even remember the last time we spoke. If Ms. Washington hadn't called me, I never would've known what happened to Janel."

"I know. I hope she's all right. I think I'm gonna to go check on her and head back to Baltimore afterward," I said, pulling out my wallet to pay for my lunch.

"You don't want to wait for me? I have a meeting this afternoon, but I'll be done by four. We can go to the hospital together."

"No, I need to get home. Thanks for letting me stay at your place. I'm glad I got to see you."

"All right, Girl. You drive safely and call me when you get home."

CHAPTER 23

Twilight Zone

The hospital looked much different in the daytime than it did the night before. It seemed a little more alive. People roamed the hallways, the receptionist was friendlier, and I actually heard sounds of laughter as I approached Janel's room.

I knocked on the door.

"Come on in," answered Ms. Washington.

I came through the door and saw Janel sitting up in her bed, looking refreshed. Ms. Washington and a young guy I didn't recognize were sitting in chairs next to Janel's bed.

"I'm glad you came back," beamed Janel. "I'm sorry I fell asleep on you last night. I guess I was really tired."

I was strangely pleased to see Janel smile.

"I'm glad to see you're doing better."

I stepped a little closer to them.

"I want you to meet Anthony," said Janel. "Anthony, this is my friend I was telling you about."

"Yes, I've heard a lot about you. It's good to finally meet you."

"Good to meet you, too." I said, and shook Anthony's hand. I had no idea who this guy was.

"Mom, could you two excuse us for a second. I want to speak to Destiny in private."

"Sure," said Ms. Washington, happy to oblige. "Anthony and I will just go get something from the cafeteria. Come on, Honey."

Anthony and Ms. Washington left the room, and I took a seat in the chair Anthony had been sitting in.

"You look much better," I said.

"I feel pretty good. It's amazing what a good night's sleep will do you for you."

I gave her a half-hearted smile.

"Thanks again for coming to see me," she said.

"Don't mention it. Vanessa should be coming up here later on. Looks like you'll be having a lot of company today."

"It seems that way. What did you think of Anthony?"

"He seems nice," I replied. I was a little annoyed that Janel was talking as though we were old friends again. Now that she had stolen my boyfriend, she had the nerve to ask me what I thought about her new one.

"Do you remember when I first told you about him?" she asked.

"No, I don't think so. I've never heard you mention that name before."

"Well, do you remember the last night we all spent together after graduation?"

"The night you left Vanessa and I at the club? Yeah, I remember that," I said with a hint of humor.

Janel gave me a guilty look.

"I'm sure you remember that it was the same night I was attacked by that group of guys. Anthony is the one who helped me get home. You told me that God had sent me an angel, even in the midst of all that mess. Remember?"

"I remember."

"That's what he was - an angel just like you." Janel cleared her throat and continued. "It was big of you to drive all the way down here to see me, especially after what I did to you. I know things will never go back to the way they used to be. I wish I could take back every ugly thing I've ever done to you and everyone else in my life that I've hurt. But I know that I can't. I'm just glad you gave me the chance to say I'm sorry."

Janel tried to fight off her tears.

"Oh, look at me," she said wiping her eye. "I'm so tired of crying." She tried to laugh away her tears.

"I want to start over, Destiny. And this is the first step. I need you to forgive me. I know I've said it many times before, but I'm ready for a change."

I closed my eyes and tried to swallow the pain that had been eating away at me ever since Janel's betrayal, no matter how hard I tried to suppress it.

"I don't know," I said listlessly. "You've put me through a lot. I'm not sure I have anything left to give you."

The corners of Janel's mouth turned south. As I looked into her glassy eyes, I knew there was no way I could come this far to go back home in the same pain I was in before I left Baltimore. The burden was too great. I wanted to be free from my feelings for Damian and free from my hatred of Janel. I only wanted good things in my life. So I had to let the bad things go.

And then His words came to me:

As God's chosen people, holy and dearly loved, clothe yourself with compassion, kindness, humility, gentleness and patience. Bear with each other and forgive whatever grievances you may have against one another. Forgive as the Lord forgave you. And over all these virtues put on love, which binds them together in perfect unity.

There was no more time for tears. It was time to push past the pain and move on.

"It hurts too bad not to forgive you, Janel," I said finally. "I need to let go of this painful grudge so I can move on with my own life. And you need my forgiveness to move on with yours. So, it's done."

"You forgive me?" she asked, hopefully.

"Yes, I forgive you. But you owe me this. You owe it to me and you owe it to yourself to honor this second chance God has given you. He obviously has special plans for your life and He didn't want you to miss out on them. Promise me you won't ever forget that."

"I promise."

I hugged Janel's warm body and kissed her soggy cheek.

"I'd better get going," I said. "Is there anything you need?"

"No, I have everything I need. I'm just ready to go home."

"When are you supposed to get out of here?"

"Probably tomorrow. My doctor wants to keep an eye on me for another day. Then he'll release me with my mother."

"Sounds good. You take care of yourself, you hear me?"

"I will. I'll never forget what you've done for me."

"Goodbye, Janel."

I left Janel's hospital room feeling like I had just stepped out of the Twilight Zone. The past 24 hours had taken me down an emotional road I didn't feel prepared to take, but I was glad it was over. As I walked down the hallway to the exit doors, my eyes caught sight of Anthony walking toward me with his arm around Ms. Washington. Janel's mother smiled when she saw me.

"Are you leaving already?" she asked as I approached them.

"Yes, ma'am. I have to get back to work."

"Okay, Honey." She reached out to hug me. "Thank you so much for driving all the way down here. I know it meant a lot to Janel. You be careful on the road, all right?"

"Okay," I said as I hugged her back.

Ms. Washington and I released our hug then I directed my attention to Anthony.

"It was nice to meet you," I said.

"Good to finally meet you, too."

"You take good care of Janel for me."

"I plan to take *very* good care of her," he said convincingly. "That's a promise."

Anthony gave me a hug then I waved a final goodbye to him and Ms. Washington.

Not long after I'd left the hospital, I found myself traveling down a series of familiar roads, and I ended up on my old college campus. I drove past the dorm where I lived my freshman year, reminiscing about all the good times I had spent there with Vanessa and Janel.

"The Modern-Day Supremes," I said to myself, smiling.

***

Exhaustion almost overtook me as I crossed the Maryland border and snaked through the miles of incessant traffic. My late night at the hospital and my early morning wake-up was starting to catch up with me. All I wanted was a bed. *Let me take that back.* All I wanted was to drive straight to J.T.'s house and collapse in his arms. And that's exactly what I did.

"There's my girl," said J.T. when he opened his apartment door. He pulled me into his embrace and squeezed me tightly before he shut the door. Then he let me go and took my jacket to hang it in the closet. "How are you feeling?" he asked.

"I'm so tired," I said wearily.

"Come on. I'll take you to bed." The next thing I knew, J.T. had picked me up in arms like a groom carrying his bride and headed toward his bedroom.

"I can't sleep here," I said, suddenly as giddy as a school girl. "I wouldn't be able to keep my hands off you."

He placed me on the bed and began taking off my shoes.

"Sure you can," he said. "I'll be a perfect gentleman." I watched J.T. pull a t-shirt out of his dresser drawer. "Here. Put this on and I'll go get your bag out of the car."

I was ready to protest, but he had already left the room. So, I took off my clothes and changed into J.T.'s t-shirt before I pulled back his covers and slid into the bed.

"Are you decent?" asked J.T., knocking on the door.

"I'm decent."

J.T. entered the bedroom and set my bag by his dresser. "How was the rest of the trip?" he asked, as he knelt onto the floor beside the bed. "You didn't seem to be doing so hot this morning."

"It was okay, actually. I'm glad I went. I was able to make some peace about a few things."

"That's good. I'm proud of you."

"Proud of me for what?" I asked, confused.

"For being you. For being where God needed you to be, even though you didn't understand why."

"Well, all I know is that I'm done with that chapter of my life, and I'm glad to have you."

"I'm glad you have me, too." He kissed the back of my hand and gazed into my face as if he hadn't seen me for months.

"I've learned a few things about forgiveness in the past few months, and I hope you can forgive me, J.T. I'm sorry if I've done anything to make you doubt me."

"I forgive you, Sweetheart. Just know that you can come to me with anything. It's all about me and you." J.T. winked at me and said, "I have something for you. It's something I should've given you a long time ago."

Uh, oh!

J.T. reached under his bed, pulled out a square-shaped box and placed it in my lap.

I covered my mouth and burst into laughs as I noticed the picture on the front of the box.

"You got me a cell phone!" I said, sounding as happy as a kid on Christmas.

"Yeah. I didn't want you to think I was trying to keep tabs on you. But I wanted you to have one. I want you to be able to call me whenever you need me, wherever you are."

I leaned toward J.T. and planted a loving kiss on his lips.

"What was that for?" he asked with a smile.

"You take such good care of me."

"There's a reason for that, Sweetheart. I love you."

His words were as soothing as balm.

"I love you, too, J.T. I've loved you for a long time. I was just too afraid to tell you."

"I never want you to be afraid of me. You can tell me anything."

"I wasn't afraid of you. I was afraid of *loving* you. But I'm not anymore. My heart is all yours if you want it."

"I promise to take good care of it," he said, convincingly.

That night, I fell asleep in J.T.'s arms, feeling more adored than I ever could've imagined. I was in love. And it felt wonderful. I finally felt free to love the way I had always wanted to – with all of me. There was nothing I had to hide - nothing to make me doubt - nothing to hold me back.

***

"I love you, Little Sister, but I am *not* sad to see you go!" joked Angel as she helped me pack my shoes into boxes.

It had been a year since I'd graduated from college and moved in with Angel. As promised, I found my own little apartment so I could move out and give her back her living space.

"I wasn't that bad of a roommate was I?"

Angel made a face.

"I'm not gonna talk about how you stay on my phone constantly, listen to the T.V. too loud or borrow my clothes all the time. Because that would make you sound like a bad roommate. So I'm not even gonna talk about all that."

"You know you're gonna miss me," I snickered.

"Maybe. But it'll be good for you to have your own place. Then you and J.T. can have some room to breathe."

"You mean so you and Walter can have some privacy!"

"That's what I said!" she cackled, and I joined in with her. "No, for real, Shutter. It's been fun having you around. I guess I will miss having you as a roommate."

The two of us continued packing until we heard the doorbell ring. Angel went to answer it, and a few moments later, J.T. came into my room wearing shorts, a white shirt and his sexy smile.

"Hey, Gorgeous," he said.

I lit up at the sight of him.

"Hello, Handsome."

I flew toward him and he picked me up in his arms like I was a baby. Before I knew it, he was laying on top of me on my bed, planting kisses all over my face. I smiled and giggled at his playfulness.

"I'm so in love with you," I said between kisses.

"I love you, too." He kissed me again. "You all packed up?"

"Almost, but I think I'd rather lay here and kiss on you all afternoon."

J.T. let his delectable lips travel down my face and onto my neck, making my breath quicken as I ran my hands over the muscles on his back.

"Hey, you two," said Angel, standing in the doorway. "There will plenty of time for all that when you're in Destiny's new apartment. Now, let's get all this crap out of here. I have plans for this bedroom," she said jokingly.

J.T. and I stood up and collected ourselves, laughing at Angel's obvious sarcasm. The three of us spent the rest of the afternoon moving furniture and boxes into my new place. I couldn't wait to decorate my apartment just the way I wanted it.

It took some time, but Angel's entrepreneurial spirit had finally rubbed off on me. That summer, I took my first steps in starting up *Destiny's Images,* my professional photography service. I took out a small business loan to buy two new cameras, two high-speed lenses, and enough lighting to set up a small studio in the spare bedroom of my apartment. I started doing more freelance work, shooting weddings, family reunions, company banquets, and I even took Jamal's high school graduation portraits. I was really beginning to come into my own.

Angel's business was steadily building, and I didn't get to spend as much time with her as I wanted. If she wasn't working, she was spending time with Walter, who I already predicted would end up being my brother-in-law. But every Sunday, Angel and I would call each other or try to meet for lunch after church.

Vanessa and Rodney ended up having a small wedding ceremony with a minister and me as the official witness. Vanessa's mother was furious, but Vanessa and Rodney had a great time consummating their marriage in Aruba.

J.T. spent the summer coaching a recreational basketball team and taking courses toward his master's degree at the University of Maryland. We spent as much time together as we could, and even took a vacation to Miami for a week. Each passing day brought us closer.

It had been an emotional struggle at times, but I loved where my new life had taken me. The past year had taught me a host of life lessons about love, friendship, sisterhood and the power of forgiveness. True enough, things didn't turn out quite the way I expected. They turned out better. But then again, God's plans always do.

EPILOGUE

One Year Later...

The sanctuary was beautiful, decorated like a scene out of heaven. Colorful flower arrangements adorned the pews and unity candles flickered in the distance as the wonder-filled crowd anxiously awaited the bride. There were no bridesmaids, no groomsmen – just Pastor Sanford and a church filled with friends and family.

I didn't think it would ever be possible, but Janel looked more beautiful than I had ever seen her. She glowed as she made her way down the aisle with her arm intertwined with that of her father. Her hour-glass figure was perfectly cased in a stunning white dress with a train as long as Rapunzel's hair.

I watched the touching ceremony unfold from a pew in the rear of the church, my hand tightly clasped with J.T.'s., Vanessa and Rodney sitting on my right. When the wedding vows were exchanged, I and every other guest in the audience couldn't keep from dropping tears.

It had been a over year since I'd seen or talked to Janel, but about six weeks ago, I received an invitation to her wedding in Angel's mail.

"Michael Davis and Gina Washington request the honor of your presence at the wedding ceremony of Janel Annette Davis and Anthony Thomas Webb," the invitation read.

I didn't call to congratulate her. I didn't even send in the R.S.V.P. card to accept or decline the invitation. But something inside me told me I should be there.

After the reading of the vows, exchanging of the rings, and the celebratory kiss, Anthony and Janel waved to their guests as they scurried back down the aisle and disappeared out of the sanctuary. The crowd rumbled and began to disperse, but several people stayed behind to get some shots during the professional photo shoot.

As usual, I was in the midst of the paparazzi with my camera in hand. Janel caught a glimpse of me snapping away, and I waved. A huge smile laced with monumental gratitude spread across her face. She waved back at me, blew me a kiss, and mouthed the words "I love you."

I felt a great sense of peace that day. I prayed that marriage would bring many happy days to Janel and Anthony. I looked over at J.T., who was waiting patiently for me to finish. I knew our day would come soon. My life felt very full, and I was thankful.

For book club discussion questions, visit

www.serenakwallace.com